THE LEGEND OF
RUSSIAN BILL

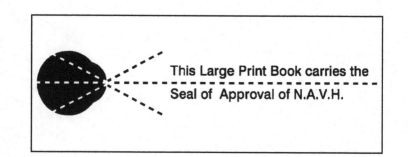

THE LEGEND OF RUSSIAN BILL

BASED ON THE REAL-LIFE STORY OF WILLIAM R. TETTENBORN

RICHARD LAPIDUS

WHEELER PUBLISHING
A part of Gale, Cengage Learning

GALE
CENGAGE Learning·

Farmington Hills, Mich • San Francisco • New York • Waterville, Maine
Meriden, Conn • Mason, Ohio • Chicago

GALE
CENGAGE Learning®

LIBRARY OF CONGRESS CATALOGING-IN-PUBLICATION DATA

Names: Lapidus, Richard, author.
Title: The legend of Russian Bill : based on the real-life story of William R. Tettenborn / by Richard Lapidus.
Description: Large print edition. | Waterville, Maine : Wheeler Publishing, a part of Gale, Cengage Learning, 2017. | Series: Wheeler Publishing large print western
Identifiers: LCCN 2017003547| ISBN 9781432838386 (softcover) | ISBN 1432838385 (softcover)
Subjects: LCSH: Outlaws—Fiction. | Large type books. | BISAC: FICTION / Historical. | FICTION / Westerns. | GSAFD: Western stories.
Classification: LCC PS3612.A6435 L44 2016b | DDC 813/.6—dc23
LC record available at https://lccn.loc.gov/2017003547

Published in 2017 by arrangement with Richard Lapidus

Printed in Mexico
1 2 3 4 5 6 7 21 20 19 18 17

This work is dedicated to my sons,
Rory, Mickey and Jamie, with love.

ACKNOWLEDGMENTS

I would like to thank the late Janaloo Hill of Shakespeare, New Mexico, and her husband, Manny Hough, who freely gave their time and research to this author, and who, despite so many obstacles, devoted their lives to keeping the historic town of Shakespeare alive and well for everyone to study and enjoy.

Special thanks go to western writers Phyllis Morreale-de la Garza and Ben T. Traywick. Others who have contributed more than they know are Henry "Buz" Lunsford, Hazel Rumney, Tiffany Schofield, Peter Zuehlke, the Tombstone, Arizona, Courthouse State Park, The Birdcage Theatre, and, of course, Irise Lapidus and the rest of my beloved family.

PREFACE

William Tettenborn, aka Russian Bill, was a
real character of the Old West. He rode a
big white horse and dressed like Buffalo
Bill. Some of his actions and activities are
recorded in documents and newspapers of
the day. Others were handed down to
pioneer families through the oral tradition.
All else is speculation. I have been fascinated
with Russian Bill's story ever since I first
heard of him while visiting Tombstone,
Arizona, in the early 1970s. I have tried to
tell his story faithfully. However, as this is a
fictional novel, certain liberties have been
taken to enhance the story.

"We know what we are but
we know not what
we may be."
William Shakespeare

CHAPTER 1

Shakespeare, New Mexico, 1881
It was Saturday night, and business was brisk at the Roxy Jay Saloon. Cowboys, miners, businessmen and fallen angels were drinking, carousing, telling high tales, and just having a spirited time.

Russian Bill peeked inside. He took a tremendous swallow from a near-empty whiskey bottle and leaned against the wall for support. His white, fringed buckskins were tattered and filthy. A bullet hole decorated his white hat. His flowing, yellow hair that he had taken so much pride in keeping clean and neatly arranged was greasy and disheveled. His fine-leather boots were dusty and scuffed. One of them had a small hole through the instep.

He shoved open the swinging doors and stood at the entrance until the conversations ceased and all eyes were on him. He growled, "I am mangy wolf from Bitter

Creek. I eat raw bear meat and stew from wildcats. I smell like dozen skunks. I weigh thousand pounds and sound of bullets whizzing by my head is favorite music."

There was an awkward stillness in the room. Then a gruff miner standing at the bar snickered. Another man howled like a wolf. Immediately everyone began laughing and returning to their previous conversations and activities.

Russian Bill tried again in a louder, drunker voice. "I am disappointed. I thought ten of you would jump up and fight. Well, that's okay. Have it your way!"

He hurled the bottle against a wall and yelled, "Watch out by door!"

He pulled a gun and blasted three holes in the already well-perforated dividing door to the gambling room. The crowd hushed and turned to watch.

"Go to hell all you Shakespeare sumbitches!"

This time he emptied the remainder of his gun and the full six shots of his other pistol, into the full-length bar mirror, shattering it, sending shards flying. Frightened and bewildered patrons dove for cover, some spilling drinks and yelling obscenities.

Russian Bill ran outside and jumped on his big, white horse. As he began to ride, the Roxy Jay bartender scrambled outside with a rifle and fired off one round. The white horse collapsed, sending Russian Bill sprawling, his wind temporarily knocked out.

He crawled back to the horse and lifted its head, stroking it with trembling hands. He quietly said, "I never tell you how much I love you. I give you plenty hard work, and you are best horse in whole world. Where you go now I don't know, but maybe I will meet you again soon."

He loaded two cartridges in his gun. One he fired in the general direction of the Roxy Jay bartender, sending him scampering back inside the saloon. Then he placed the gun barrel against his own temple, and, still stroking the horse's head, he closed his eyes. He held it that way for a few seconds and then jammed the gun back into its holster while muttering something in Russian. He quickly removed pouches of gold, a blanket roll and canteen from the up side of the dead horse. He crawled to a hitching rail and secured his belongings on the one horse that had turned to watch him approach, a handsome black.

Once in the saddle, he spurred it and galloped out of town just as Avon Street began to fill with spectators.

CHAPTER 2

16 Months Earlier
Tombstone, Arizona

It was the best day in the life of prospector Tom Waters, and the worst day. In poker he had pulled four aces and a king-ten full house. In faro his numbers kept coming up time and time again. Everything came up roses for him that warm spring day.

After a while he started drinking. Even that hadn't changed his luck. But Tom Waters was a mean drunk and he became abusive with those he gambled with, including the dealers and even the bartenders. Several times he was reminded that he was on a winning streak. He should remember that and lighten up. But he didn't.

There came a time when boredom set in, even as the cards kept falling his way. He went outside and lit a cigar. He noticed a merchandise store across the street and he witnessed a woman coming out with a package. He considered that he should buy himself something, so he walked across the street and entered the store to see what he could find.

Twenty minutes later Waters exited the store wearing a new shirt in the pattern of a bright blue and black checkerboard. The pattern and bright colors were so new and different to the miners, cowboys, and businessmen, that when Waters crossed their path, they all felt compelled to make a comment. These comments were not necessarily meaning any harm, but Waters, being drunk and grumpy, was not in the mood for either compliments or criticisms, no matter how innocent or well-intentioned they might have been.

A miner happened to exit a saloon on Allen Street when Waters approached. "Whoa," he said looking at the shirt. Waters held his tongue but stamped his boot down hard on the boards. Then he stagger-bumped into a skinny cowboy out in the street. The cowboy stepped back and took a look at Waters. He snickered under his breath and shielded his eyes. Waters observed this and kicked up a cloud of dust at the cowboy, who had already crossed the street.

While Waters was still staggering around

in his own dust cloud, a donkey cart almost crashed into him. Waters became enraged and yelled, "You almost ran into me, you crazy sumbitch!"

The driver going by yelled back, "Sorry, mister, but yer shirt is blinding my ass!"

But Waters kept drinking and getting drunker and meaner. The comments about the shirt didn't stop coming. Finally, over at Corrigan's saloon, Waters downed his whiskey, turned away from the bar and addressed the customers. He said, "I'm sick and tired of hearing gossip about this shirt. Starting now any man that don't like this shirt, let him say so and I will knock him down."

Immediately after making that speech a friend of his named Bradshaw came in. Bradshaw and Waters at one time had shared a house and they had prospected together, so they were more than casual acquaintances. Bradshaw ordered his whiskey. That's when he noticed the shirt. He looked over at Waters and said, "Kinda loud, ain't it?"

Immediately and without warning, Waters shot Bradshaw a powerful right hook above the left eye. Bradshaw, having no indication that this was coming, went down unconscious.

Tom Waters left Corrigan's and started arguments and fights all over town. Bradshaw went home and grabbed his pistol. It was easy for him to locate Waters. All he had to do was follow the noise and the crowd.

Bradshaw came up on Waters. "Why did you hit me?" he asked. Waters responded with a fusillade of cussing and threats. Bradshaw, whose head was still throbbing where a sizable lump had emerged, turned to a miner he knew and said, "Did you hear those threats?" The miner affirmed that he had, as had at least twenty others in the immediate vicinity. Bradshaw removed his pistol and shot Waters four times, killing him before he hit the ground.

Bradshaw was arrested, but he was soon released when witness after witness came forward who had heard the threats.

This incident brought excitement to the camp. For several days people spoke of Waters, the shirt, the threats, and the killing. They spoke of the fine run of luck Waters had with the cards and the ultimate bad luck he had because of his poor taste in shirts and a horrible temper. They reminisced about the jarring right hook that sent Bradshaw to the floor, and what a tragedy and shame it was for a friendship to end like that.

When the excitement ended in the saloons, in the mines, in the shops, and on the street, a lull of quiet came over Tombstone. People were waiting for something to happen. Therefore no one was disappointed a few days later when Russian Bill came to town.

CHAPTER 3

Russian Bill walked through the elegantly furnished hotel lobby of the Cosmopolitan Hotel on Allen Street. As he approached the registration desk, a clerk looked up and froze. Sheriff John Behan sat on a plush couch reading a newspaper. He had caught a glimpse of the oddly-dressed stranger as he walked by, but the sheriff now had to crane his neck, as his view was obstructed by a structural column.

Russian Bill addressed the clerk. "My good man, may I into my confidence take you?"

The fully astonished clerk said, "Yes, sir."

Russian Bill did some hocus-pocus and came up with a coin from behind the clerk's ear. He plopped it on the counter.

"Do you an outlaw named Curly Bill Brocius know?"

The clerk leaned down and talked softly. "Yes, sir, everybody knows who he is. I don't know him personally." He reached down and secured the coin in his vest pocket.

Russian Bill produced another coin from behind the clerk's other ear, and he set it on the counter. Sheriff Behan tried to see what was going on without being obvious. The clerk thumbed through the ledger. He scratched his head.

"Mr. Brocius, John Ringo and a couple of the Clanton Brothers stayed here last time they were in town. See right here: they all signed their names. That was two, no, three weeks ago. But mister, may I ask what your business is with Curly Bill?"

Russian Bill smiled. "Of course you may ask, sir. You have most cooperative been so far, so I will right now tell that I have a very long way come for which to up join, and with Curly Bill and his gang of outlaws will soon ride."

The clerk thought about this and then said, "You might ride down to Charleston. I hear he sometimes hangs out down there."

Russian Bill was puzzled. "Charleston? Isn't that in Carolina where ocean meets? That very long ride is."

"No, sir, this Charleston is south of here." He picked up the second coin from the counter and nonchalantly paired it up with the first one in his vest pocket.

This time Russian Bill simply plunked down another coin without any flourish. The clerk closed the ledger. "See, the silver is here in Tombstone, but there's no water here to run a mill to refine it. So, yonder on the east side of the San Pedro River is Millville, where the mill is situated, and on the west side is Charleston, where the workers live. The Clanton Ranch is right close so . . ."

He noticed that Russian Bill had turned away to stare at the man behind the newspaper.

Russian Bill turned back to the clerk. "If you please, would you a room with a view of the street to me give?"

The clerk said, "Yes, sir. How long will you be staying?"

"That depends," said Russian Bill placing a large gold coin on the counter. "I, that this, will my bill satisfy for some time trust."

The clerk picked up the coin and examined it briefly. He pushed the ledger and an inkwell and pen across the counter. Then he handed Russian Bill a key. "Sign here, please, sir. Up the stairs, third door on the right."

Russian Bill signed the ledger, took the key, and walked up the stairs.

Sheriff Behan folded and set down the newspaper, walked to the stairwell, looked up to make sure the coast was clear, then stepped over to the registration desk. "What did that fancy dude want?" he asked.

"It's the queerest thing. Far as I can make out he wants to find Curly Bill so he can join his gang. And look at this." He showed Sheriff Behan the gold coin. "He paid for his room with a twenty-dollar gold piece."

Behan said, "What did you say?"

"He paid with a . . ."

"No," Behan said. "Something about Curly Bill."

"Oh, yeah," the clerk said. "He said he wants to find Curly Bill and join his gang. He sure talks funny."

"That foreigner sumbitch wants to join Curly Bill's gang? That's rich. What's the dude's name?"

The clerk opened the ledger again and slid it over.

Sheriff Behan stared at the writing in disbelief. "What the . . . ? What in the hell kind of writing is that?"

CHAPTER 4

He was the most unusual man many citizens of Tombstone had ever seen. When he walked into the Eagle Brewery he stood straight and tall inside the doors, bright-blue eyes searching around the room. His long, wavy, yellow hair fell below the shoulders of his white, fringed, buckskin shirt, and his pure-white hat had no sweat stains. His fine-leather boots had high heels and fancy tops, which he wore with the buckskin pants tucked inside. Huge spurs jingled whenever he took a step, especially on the boarded sidewalks along Allen and Fremont Streets. His guns were pearl-handled Colts, and when he got close you couldn't miss the four precisely carved notches on one of the handles. His brown, tooled-leather belt was filled with cartridges.

He stood with his hands close to those guns and peered around the room with a scowl on his face, as if studying everyone and warning them at the same time. The customers and staff were helpless to do anything but stare. He proceeded to the bar and sidled up nice and cozy to it, running his hands along the smooth, mahogany surfaces. He immediately ordered whiskey, and then turned away from the bar to address all those who were staring. He spoke in a language that was clearly English, but the words and the word order were at times very different from the frontier style that nearly everyone spoke in the mining camps. To complicate matters even more, he also articulated in a kind of a throaty monotone rather than the singsong and melodious rhythms of the day.

"Captain William R. Tettenborn my name is. I am an outlaw by the name of Brocius, Curly Bill Brocius, looking for."

A miner named Scott, who ironically was from Wales, finished his drink and stood up to leave when he heard Curly Bill's name mentioned. Russian Bill, who still called himself William R. Tettenborn at that time, stopped him.

"Please do not, sir, yet to leave." He looked around the room, taking care to make eye contact with everyone. "Has anyone Curly Bill Brocius seen?"

Scott the miner froze. There was silence

in the Eagle Brewery, and nobody moved.

Russian Bill spoke right up again. "That too bad is. I had to buy him drink tonight hoped, and with him a long talk to have had."

Everyone looked at his drinking neighbor for possible clues to what this odd stranger had said, but only head shakes and shrugs were seen.

Then Russian Bill announced, "And now, since Curly Bill drinking with not going to happen is, may I pleasure have to please everyone here a drink buying?"

Funny how everyone understood that language, especially Scott, who suddenly came to life with a wide grin, and no longer wanted to leave. Russian Bill tossed a gold coin on the bar, which the bartender picked up and studied. Then whiskey was poured for everyone. When Russian Bill's glass was filled, he leaned back and downed the dark amber liquid in one swallow. Immediately a completely dissatisfied look contorted his face.

He addressed the bartender. "Please, my fine fellow. In my country I am nobleman. I the good stuff require."

The bartender reached for another bottle, a full one, which he opened and poured for Russian Bill. Russian Bill fished out an elaborate, hand-carved comb, and began to run it through his long, yellow, wavy hair while scrutinizing the newly poured liquid. He lifted the glass, held it up to his eyes for a couple seconds, and then downed the whiskey with a twist of his wrist and a wink of an eye. He gritted his teeth, set down the glass hard on the bar, and let out a long satisfying hiss.

He looked up at the bartender and said, "That's, that's more okay. Very kind of you. Now please a cigar for me to get."

The bartender started to reach on a shelf to pull one out of a half-empty box, but Russian Bill watched him and interrupted the process by saying, "A good cigar!"

Several customers, mainly miners, who had recently come in straight from their mid-shift, delighted with their free drinks and with the antics of the curious stranger in their midst, smiled or whispered to one another as they observed the bartender reach into another box on the shelf.

"Very kind of you," Russian Bill said as he accepted the perfecto. Everyone was talking quietly while watching to see what this Tettenborn fellow was going to do next, when the sound of approaching horses was heard.

CHAPTER 5

Russian Bill turned to the swinging doors and lit his cigar as three cowboys entered and swaggered up to the bar. All of a sudden the one who acted like the leader noticed Russian Bill standing there in his white, fringed clothing.

"Whoa, Nellie," he said. "What in the world? Mister, I am a hard man from Bitter Creek. I smell like a mangy wolf, I eat bear meat, and the whine of bullets going by is my favorite music. I don't know who or what you are, but . . ." Here he paused and noticed that all eyes in the room were on him. Russian Bill was silently mouthing some words, as if he were trying to remember something. The customers were absorbed in the dialogue, wondering if a bar fight was about to begin.

The cowboy leader continued. "As I was saying, I don't know who or what you are, but I like yer style, so stay where y'are an' nominate yer pizen."

Before Russian Bill could say anything, the bartender, who seemed to know these men, said, "This here is Captain William R. Tettenborn. He's looking for Curly Bill, and he just bought everyone a drink."

Russian Bill made a little bow, and the bartender poured drinks for the three cowboys, and with a sweep of his hand and a finger pointing at Russian Bill, it was understood that these were part of Russian Bill's tab. The bartender, being a fair man, then refilled Russian Bill's glass and indicated in a similar manner that the cowboy leader was paying for that one.

The leader stared hard at Russian Bill and rubbed his chin whiskers. "Tettenborn, Tettenborn. Nope. I don't b'lieve I've heard of you before."

The three cowboys were standing at the bar, side by side, and the middle one, who was slender and tall and wore a grubby hat, leaned over and whispered something in the leader's ear. The leader motioned for another drink by pointing to their three empty glasses, and Russian Bill's.

As the whiskey was being poured the leader said, "My friend here thinks he might o' seen you down to Shakespeare."

Russian Bill was about to say something,

but before he could get in a word, the tall, slender cowboy leaned over and whispered something else, which caused the leader to give the tall cowboy a disgusted look, as he removed his neck scarf and wiped off his wet ear. Then he said, "My friend also wants to know what kind of name is Tattenbaum, and he's also a mite curious what you want with Curly Bill."

Russian Bill smiled, downed his whiskey, and walked around, stopping to face the three cowboys. "Tetten-born," he said. "I need to Curly Bill locate so I can with his gang of outlaws join. And please to excuse me mister cowboy who whispers, there a real town named Shakespeare is?"

The three cowboys all nodded affirmatively.

"Shakespeare," said Russian Bill. "What a delightful name for a western town is. You know it the bard William Shakespeare was himself who spoke of names through Romeo. *By a name I know not how to tell you who I am. My name, dear saint, is hateful to myself, because it is an enemy to thee. Had I it written, I would tear the word.* No, gentlemen, my name is Tettenborn, and I not yet the pleasure of Shakespeare the town visiting have had. But soon I hope go."

Over the head of the third cowboy, the

shortest of the gang, Russian Bill noticed his reflection in the bar mirror. He removed his hat, yanked out his comb again, and began running it through his hair, to the silent amusement of everyone in the room.

CHAPTER 6

After three days and nights in Tombstone, Russian Bill was ready to head to Charleston, where several people told him that Curly Bill liked to hang out. He had made a considerable amount of friends, as a rivulet of whiskey had been poured at his pleasure and expense. Even so, he was not without a share of detractors. When he had been either happy or melancholy from the effects of the whiskey, he told of his royal Russian lineage, of the generals and dignitaries he had met, and the acts of bravery he had committed. Only a few of Tombstone's citizens had taken a supporting position, that it was within the realm of possibility that these statements were true. Most considered Russian Bill to be a peculiar character whose main eccentricities were bragging and lying.

Although Russian Bill had been the main topic of conversation in Tombstone, as Tom

Waters and his too-bright shirt had been before him, Russian Bill's pure-white horse had also garnered a fair share of gossip. Not only was the perfect, solid-white color most unusual in the mining camp, but the horse was tall, standing at over seventeen hands. And Russian Bill had taught the horse a few tricks, such as pawing the dirt, bowing and neighing.

People everywhere marveled at Russian Bill and his horse. And he was almost always willing to stop and put on a little demonstration. He had just come out of the combination general store and Agency Pima County Bank with a heavy saddlebag. A banker accompanied him to his horse. He carefully placed the leather bags on his horse and began running his comb through the horse's mane. Then he removed his hat and ran the comb through his yellow hair. A small crowd had gathered to watch, and, within a short time, the spectators were all smiles and giggles.

Russian Bill tipped his hat, swung himself onto the horse, and rode south toward Charleston. It would be a long time before he would be replaced as the most worthy topic of conversation in Tombstone.

The water level in the San Pedro River was

high. Russian Bill had decided to take a bath and was standing buck naked in the water, looking at the reflection of his hair and wondering why the flow of the water was heading north instead of south as in most other rivers. The horse was standing at the bank with his head lowered, taking a long drink.

Russian Bill noticed the horse lift his head, perk up his ears, and take a few steps backward. Then he heard gunshots and horses frantically approaching. In the distance he saw a lone rider being pursued in his direction by three Apaches. The rider was firing a rifle over the shoulder, and the Apaches were shooting arrows.

From a distance the rider yelled to Russian Bill, "Hey, mister, a little help here, please!"

Russian Bill froze for a moment, but when an arrow screamed by his ear, he scrambled out of the water and over to the horse. He yanked his rifle from its sheath, aimed steady, and held his position until he was sure of the shot.

When a second arrow flew by Russian Bill's neck, it sent the blood pumping fast and hard through his body. He yelled, *"Govno!"* and squeezed the trigger. Instantly the closest Apache went down hard. The two other Indians stopped and retreated. Russian Bill fired again but missed. The two uninjured Apaches cautiously dragged their companion off and rode away.

The rider dismounted, stared at Russian Bill a moment, and then began speaking. "Thanks, mister. For a while there I thought I was gonna be a free lunch for the coyotes."

Russian Bill, in his strange accent and word order, replied, "Those Apaches were?"

"Those Apaches were what? Hey, mister, I don't want to sound ungrateful, but do you have any clothes that you could put on?"

Russian Bill was in a bit of a daze. When he looked down and saw that he was naked, he said *"Govno"* again and scrambled to the riverbank, where he had neatly folded his clothes. He dressed himself quickly.

The rider said, "Hey, mister, where are you from? I'm not familiar with that word, *govno,* which I believe I heard you shout twice."

"I am long way from here come," said Russian Bill. "Russia from. *Govno* it means of concern expression. Not polite word. I, sir, apologize. You, Apaches by surprise take me."

The rider smiled while calculating the meaning of these words. "Seems like there's many surprises out here today. The 'paches are no surprise. They fight with us, with the Mexicans, and even with other tribes. But you, finding someone like you out here, well, I'm about as surprised as a slut dog with her first porcupine to find a naked-as-a-jaybird Russian standing in the San Pedro River. I'm glad you're handy with that rifle is all. Even though it seemed to take forever for you to get off a shot."

Russian Bill buttoned up the last of his white buckskins and smiled at the rider. "I, sir, on several occasions my man got, and doing this, as the poet said, *wisely and slow. They stumble that run fast.*" He was dressed at that point and unmindfully began fussing with his hair.

"Well," said the rider, "the grass is waving over many fellers who pulled the trigger without aiming. But if you'll take my advice, try and get off a good shot a smidgen quicker next time, and if you feel like expressing a concern, say *shit.* Say, you sure got purty hair. If you don't mind me asking, how do you keep it so nice out here in this desert?"

Russian Bill did not mind talking about his hair. In fact, he loved to. "It time takes," he said. "I castile soap and lavender oil mix. In St. Louis I a supply have purchased, and at least one time each week must wash."

The rider had never heard of anyone washing their hair that often, and thus shot Russian Bill a quizzical look, while at the same time removing her hat and allowing her flowing, brown hair to fall below her waist. And she ran her fingers through it.

Russian Bill stared in amazement, realizing for the first time that this was a woman dressed in men's clothes. Then he remembered that he had just stood naked in front of her. He turned away, embarrassed, and said, "*Govno,* shit."

Before long the lady rider and Russian Bill found a shady spot under a tree. There they ate dried beef, which the lady provided, and hard biscuits, which he had brought along on his ride to Charleston. They ate, drank water from their canteens, and talked.

"Say, what's your name, mister?"

"I William R. Tettenborn name is. Captain in Russian Imperial Guards was used to be. What your name is, please?"

"Pleased to meet you, William. My name is Lana. Lana Harris."

Russian Bill studied her features. "Lana, that Russian is, no? In Russia we have Svetlana, meaning of light. Svetlana, light. You have family from maybe Russia come?"

"I don't think so," she said. "Not unless they moved Dublin out of Ireland. What are you doing out here in that crazy outfit?"

"Crazy? Perhaps, it more better is to why you dress like man ask."

Lana smiled and took some water from her canteen.

"Were you in the basement when they handed out brains, William? What would the 'paches do if they saw a woman wearing a dress, long hair flowing down, riding sidesaddle? Or the Mexicans who come up here to steal back the cattle we stole from them? Or . . . but that doesn't explain what you're doing naked in the river or dressed like Buffalo Bill Cody in this 'pache and outlaw country."

Russian Bill lowered his head. "Well, you, yes about basement must be right. I very stupid shooting Indians with family jewels waving like Russian flag am. For you, to have seen I am sad and ashamed."

This softened Lana. She relaxed and smiled. "Don't be silly, William. You had no way of knowing. Besides, you saved my life."

Russian Bill began to reply, but then realized he had both biscuit and dried beef in his mouth. It presented a dilemma, but he clearly wanted to talk more than he wanted to eat, so he nonchalantly removed his neck scarf and casually used it to transfer the partially chewed wad of food from his mouth.

"As for Buffalo Bill, I him meet. We talk. Also General named Philip Sheridan. I him salute, shake hand, we talk. And lieutenant named George Armstrong Custer. He long, yellow hair have, but maybe mine better is. Also President Ulysses S. Grant. We talk. Spotted Tail, Chief of Lakota Sioux Indian Tribe. We talk. And Two Lance, Chief of Nakotas. We all buffalo hunt go."

Lana had somewhere to go. Besides that, she was crazy confused about what Russian Bill had just told her. She mounted her pony and turned to address Russian Bill. "I enjoyed the picnic, William, but I have a couple words of advice. First off, I wouldn't tell anyone else about your adventures with Grant and them others. And second, dammit, move the verb after the noun, or put it anywhere but the last word in the sentence. Makes me want to scream. Gotta go now. This feller got thrown and kicked by a stallion and probably got a broken leg. Gotta fetch a doctor. There's a few of them in Tombstone."

As she started to urge her horse away, Russian Bill shouted at her, "I five languages speak."

Lana pulled her horse to a stop and

turned to face Russian Bill one final time. "Better to speak one or two correctly. Listen, what you said. 'I five languages speak.' It's simple. Just say, 'I speak five languages.' Don't put the verb at the end of the sentence. If you're wondering why I'm so smart about the English language, my daddy was a lawyer, and he made sure all six of his children had an education. Goodbye, William."

CHAPTER 7

Once in Charleston, it did not take Russian Bill long to discover that Curly Bill had already left the area. So he got himself in a poker game to pass the time and figure out his next move. Also in the game were four rough-looking characters named Vaughan, Johnson, Mitchell, and Downs. He was only playing a few minutes when he ordered whiskey for the table.

The bartender filled five glasses with whiskey and put them on a tray. When he got to the table, the cowboy named Vaughan stuck his foot out and the bartender stumbled, sending the tray of drinks right into Russian Bill, who immediately jumped up to wipe himself off. During the commotion he noticed Vaughan doing some fancy card switching.

The cowboy called Johnson thought Russian Bill had stood up to pound on the bartender for spilling the drinks and soiling his buckskins. Johnson stood up and yelled, "Please don't shoot the bartender, mister. He's about as awkward as a blind bear in a bramble patch, but he didn't mean anything by it."

Russian Bill stroked his yellow mustache. "I have no intention of the bartender shooting. I mean I have no intention of shooting the bartender. Accidents happen. However one of you have cheated at this poker. I have observed this, and I will certainly kill anyone who tries to gain unfair advantage by cheating. I know you are some rough fellows. Maybe you think because I am from other country that I fall off lettuce wagon. But you don't know me or what I have done to others who chose to fight. I offer you my word as a gentleman and as an outlaw, soon to ride with Curly Bill, that I will shoot you in the heart if you cheated at this game and do not this very instant get up and leave your chips, which you have forfeit by act of cheating, and leave saloon."

Russian Bill knew that Vaughan had cheated, but he didn't know about any others. So he was surprised when Vaughan stood up, and then, one by one, so did Johnson, Mitchell, and Downs. They all quickly left the saloon without reaching for any chips.

Only the bartender was looking his way when Russian Bill surveyed the room. He gathered up the considerable spread of chips and brought them to the bar, keeping an eye on the swinging doors to make sure none of the cheaters came back in looking for trouble.

"I'm sorry about that, sir," the bartender said. "That one fella, Vaughan, stuck his foot out and . . ."

"That is fine, my good man. That stunt is known to me as diversion. Whenever there is diversion it usually means something else is happening shouldn't be. Now, please, everyone I speak to says Curly Bill is no longer here in Charleston. Is that correct?"

The bartender glanced around and answered in a whisper. "Few days ago Curly Bill, John Ringo and the Clanton Brothers parked themselves in here for two days. I tell you it was all I could do to find time to go to the outhouse."

Russian Bill asked him if he knew where Curly Bill could be now. The bartender offered that Galeyville over in the Chiricahua Mountains was another of Curly Bill's hangouts. He said it would be a little out of the way, but he might go through Willcox. Someone there might have seen him. He should take the trail over the Dragoon

Mountains. When he comes out on the other side, he should ride in the direction of two giant rocks in the northeast mountains. If he heads for them he will find Willcox easy enough.

Russian Bill thanked him and, pointing to the big pile of chips on the bar, said that since he had been successful at poker, could he have the pleasure of buying the bartender a drink?

The bartender poured one for each of them and said, "I sure hope you know what you're doing, mister. With Curly Bill, I mean. Rub him the wrong way and he will kill you as sure as coyotes howl."

Suddenly shouts and shots were heard out in the street. Random bullets were breaking lamps and windows and zinging through thin, clapboard storefronts. One bullet broke the whiskey bottle the bartender was holding and another creased Russian Bill's buckskin shirt, tearing off some fringe. Still another broke the bar glass. The few remaining patrons dove for cover. Russian Bill crawled to the back door. Once outside he heard somebody shouting that Sandy King was shooting up the town.

Meanwhile, out on the street, Sandy King was rough-riding his horse this way and that, howling like an angry wolf and shooting up the town. When he rode to the end of the street, where a new building was under construction, a man wearing a badge swung a big plank board and knocked Sandy King off his horse, with Sandy vomiting on the way down and landing smack in its midst.

By the time Sandy King was behind bars, Russian Bill was riding out of Charleston. On this dark, moonless night, he had no idea who Sandy King was or the substantial problems the two of them would face together not too far down the trail.

CHAPTER 8

On his way to Willcox, Russian Bill had crossed the Dragoon Mountains on a wagon trail and emerged into a grassy valley when he saw a bunch of buzzards circling. He considered that this was most likely due to a dead cow or horse, but then he wondered why, if this were the case, the big birds were still in the air. He decided to take a quick detour and see what was what, and he rode with great haste to the area below the black moving circle.

He soon came upon some trampled grass, then cow patties. Riding around he discovered blood drippings in the grass. Up ahead he found a cowboy on the ground, face up, bleeding from the side. Russian Bill quickly rode up to the man and looked down on him from the saddle.

The cowboy was Ned Warner. He looked up through teary eyes and saw Russian Bill, dressed all in white on top of his big, white horse. Ned contemplated, and then gulped out, "You are Saint Peter coming to take me aloft."

Russian Bill looked down on him and replied in a gentle voice, "No, my friend, I am not Saint Peter, but I am from St. Petersburg."

The wounded cowboy blinked and tried to clear his head. "Is that what y'all call it up there?"

Russian Bill dismounted and looked down.

Ned Warner tried to sit up. "Do you have anything to drink? I'm so thirsty I'll even drink water. Are you sure you're not Saint Pete, 'cause I gotta say, mister, I'm mighty glad to see you and all, but dressed up in that white suit on that big, white horse, you look like you come down to saddle me to a cloud and ride me up to the great beyond. And I don't mind telling you that this is one big surprise to me as I've thought for a long time now that I'm a-going to the other place. Say, they didn't send you here to trick me, did they?"

Russian Bill grabbed his canteen and handed it to Ned Warner. He looked down at the wound. "What happened here?"

"I got bushwhacked by some Mezkins. Shot me clear off my horse. Stole 'im too.

And they rustled the cows I was moving."

Russian Bill walked to his horse and pulled a blanket down from where he had it rolled behind the saddle. He cut long strips with a Bowie knife. Then he wrapped Ned Warner's side wound tightly.

"Are we going to St. Petersburg now?" Ned Warner asked.

As Russian Bill hoisted him up in the saddle and positioned himself behind him, he said, "To the Imperial Capital of Russia? That is very long ride. I cannot go there. I am outlaw there. Soon I will be outlaw here. In your condition I think it will be better if we ride into Willcox and see about a doctor."

Hearing that, Ned Warner blinked and thought about it for a few seconds. "A doctor? You mean, you mean I'm gonna live?"

"You are tough cowboy. I think you will live. Lots of blood come out, but look like bullet go all the way through. But you must want to live and believe it will happen."

Russian Bill cluck-clucked and urged the big, white horse southeast toward Willcox. After a few minutes Ned Warner said, "Curly Bill is gonna be so upset."

Russian Bill stopped the horse. "You know him, Curly Bill?"

Ned Warner squirmed a bit. "Know him?

Those were his beeves I was moving. Um, um, um, he's gonna be ringy, riled, on the prod, on the peck, have his bristles up, and . . ."

As they finally arrived in Willcox, Russian Bill had kept Ned Warner alert by continually talking to him. They had introduced each other by name, and Ned thought that Tettenborn was a funny kind of name for a man to carry around. They had talked about Curly Bill, and Ned suggested that Curly most likely would be found in Galeyville, as the bartender in Charleston had advised.

Ned Warner told of the Clanton Brothers and John Ringo and other good men that society would most likely classify as outlaws. Russian Bill was highly interested and wanted to hear more, but he was beginning to get nervous about the amount of blood that Ned Warner had lost. Ned was also beginning to get delirious.

"Say mister, and 'scuse me for not remembering your name, wherever it is that yer taking me, are we almost there, 'cause I'm not feeling too good. I think I'm starting to see angels flying by."

Russian Bill had to raise his voice. "Listen to me, Ned. We are here. Hang on. You've got to believe me. You will live if you want to. Please hang on."

As fate would have it, Russian Bill saw a shingle reading *James Morse, M.D.* hanging on a house around the corner from a busy saloon called Foxey's. He dismounted, caught the cowboy as he slid out of the saddle, and carried him to the front door of the house. "Emergency! Emergency! Emergency!" he yelled and pounded on the door.

When the door opened, Russian Bill carried Ned Warner inside.

CHAPTER 9

Deep in the mountains, Curly Bill Brocius and an associate named Jim Wallace had arrived in Galeyville and were entering their favorite hangout, the Gem Saloon.

The Gem was nothing like any saloon in Tombstone, unless you went back to the earliest days in the camp when all businesses were in tents while the town was being built. This was very basic, with a wide board resting on barrels and covered with oilcloth standing as the bar. There were a few tables and chairs. When Curly Bill and Jim Wallace entered, there were two Indians sitting on a bench, and two drunk freighters were sitting in a corner. The freighters alternated between quietly arguing with each other and laughing. At the bar stood a half-drunk soldier and a mountain man with pelts on his person and on the floor next to his two hunting dogs. Behind the bar stood a lanky man named Jeff Logan, who was bent over fiddling with some receipts.

Curly Bill wore rough pants stuck in his boots, a blue shirt, red neck scarf, a large hat with the front brim turned up, a Bowie knife in his boot, and two six-shooters on his waist. Jim Wallace dressed less gaudy and more regular for a cowboy who rode the range. As soon as he entered the Gem, Curly Bill exchanged pleasantries with Jeff Logan and called for drinks for everyone. But when he looked around, he modified his request to exclude the two Indians.

"Hey, you Indians, get out now!" he said.

The Indians got up slowly. They were too old to either protest or fight. When the Indians stood up, the hunting dogs also got up and began barking. One of the Indians walked right outside. The other started to leave, but stopped to address the barking dogs. He glared at them, made a scary face, and brought up a chilling growl from deep within. Then he exited to catch up to his companion. The dogs cowered against the mountain man's legs and whimpered.

This process captured Curly Bill's attention, and he addressed the mountain man. "You, wearing all those dead squirrels, these your dogs?"

"Yes, indeedy," the mountain man replied. "Finest pair of coonhounds I ever known."

Curly Bill snickered. "Look more like squirrel hounds to me. The way these two just cowered and cried from that tired ol' Indian, whatcha gonna do if you track a bear or a lion? Why these two would run like hell if the bear stood up or the lion screamed."

The mountain man looked down and muttered something about how he had never seen them act like that before, and he hoped they weren't permanently damaged by that ghostly Indian growl.

Jeff Logan went around the room pouring whiskey.

CHAPTER 10

After depositing Ned Warner at the doctor's house, Russian Bill asked all around Willcox for any sightings of Curly Bill. By purchasing a few rounds of drinks in Foxey's, he confirmed that Curly Bill would most likely be in Galeyville when he arrived there. He thought it was too soon to check on Ned Warner's condition, so he staked himself to some grub at a restaurant on Railroad Avenue while the big, white horse had oats and a brushing at the livery down the street.

Then, heading southeast toward the Chiricahuas Mountains, Russian Bill passed the thriving gold and silver mines at Dos Cabezas, named for the two house-size boulders that resembled bald heads in the mountains. Galeyville, he had been told, was located high up in a pine forest on the eastern side of the Chiricahuas.

Russian Bill rode through Pinery Canyon

on a narrow section of trail, and was approaching the summit when a rider came out from the trees and began descending toward him. The rider was Jim Hughes, a young friend of Curly Bill's. Both riders stopped their horses almost nose to nose to avoid a forced detour off the trail.

Jim Hughes chuckled at the sight of Russian Bill. "Well, look at the fancy dude. What are you dressed up for, stranger, a show or something? You going to a show? Are you an actor? They got a theater in Tombstone, but you're riding the wrong way. Say, are you lost or somethin'?"

Russian Bill glared at the young cowboy but said nothing.

Jim Hughes shrugged. "What's the matter? I thought actors like to talk. Why don't you recite something fancy to go along with your outfit?"

Russian Bill smiled as thoughts were racing through his head. He removed his hat, set it on his lap momentarily, and ran his fingers through his long, curly hair. He carefully placed the hat back on his head and recited, *All the world's a stage, and all the men and women merely players; they have their exits and their entrances; and one man in his time plays many parts . . ."*

"Hey, I was right. You are an actor, and a

good one. That was downright inspirational. Kind of inspires me to play a part. Bet you can't guess what kind of part." Jim Hughes chuckled again.

Russian Bill had a feeling about the situation that was evolving on the trail. Behind the young cowboy he watched two jays squawking at a squirrel and chasing it out of a tree. The squirrel scampered to the ground, paused to look up at the two men and the two horses, determined quickly that it wanted none of that, and ran halfway up another pine, a few trees away from the noisy birds.

Russian Bill decided that he would stay on guard and not be knocked off course. He stared at Jim Hughes. "You are quite right, young sir. Now, if you'll kindly allow me to pass, I must be on my way."

Jim Hughes did not budge. He instantly replied, "You see, I'm an actor, too. Ain't that a peach? Two actors meeting on a trail like this, nobody else around. 'Course I'm just learning, so I don't have any speeches memorized, or costumes, and . . . but wait. Now that I think of it, I do have one. See, in this play I'm a horse trader. I meet some dude on the trail and I say . . . well, first I pull my gun and aim at his head, kind of like this."

He wasted no time in demonstrating the movement. "Then I say, 'That's a fine looking horse you have there, stranger. I'm a horse trader so I believe I'll trade horses with you. And I will charge you a transaction fee of five dollars.' "

Russian Bill shifted his position in the saddle. "Yes, not Shakespeare but very convincing. Just like I think an outlaw would say."

Jim Hughes nodded. "Glad to hear it. Now get down off your horse and uncinch your saddle."

Russian Bill expected that something like this would happen, so he was somewhat prepared. He slowly climbed down off his horse, thinking all the time.

Jim Hughes had Russian Bill sized up as a harmless actor, a dude dressed up for a show. In that misjudgment he had tucked his pistol into his belt and started to uncinch his own saddle. That's when he heard a familiar click. When he looked up he saw Russian Bill standing calmly, a grin on his face, aiming his gun at Hughes's heart. He watched as Russian Bill pulled the hammer back. And he noticed that the hand that leveled the gun at him was steady.

"Say, what in the world?" Jim Hughes said with surprise and disappointment.

Russian Bill pulled on the ends of his mustache. "Put back your saddle on. It is time for you, my young outlaw bad actor friend, to make exit before I let sunshine come through you."

The young outlaw shook his head and glared at Russian Bill. Then he went about the business of cinching back up his saddle and mounting his horse. "I'll get you for this, you queer-talking foreigner son-of-a-bitch."

Russian Bill chuckled. The scene had played out just as he pictured it would. Curly Bill himself would have been proud of the way he had handled himself. "In any language, the whine of a bullet is big hint."

Jim Hughes sat in the saddle seething. His fair complexion had turned red. "I promise you, if we meet up again, there won't be no hints." He spurred his horse and rubbed up against Russian Bill and his horse as he headed down the trail.

Russian Bill called after him, "You should enlist in army, sonny. You'd make fine soldier the way you take orders so good."

Russian Bill watched him head down the trail, then cluck-clucked and said *"Payehali"* to his horse, which is Russian for *let's go.* Then he rode over the ridge through the pine trees back on his way to Galeyville.

CHAPTER 11

John Galey opened the Texas Mine when silver was discovered in the Chiricahua Mountains. Being a successful Pennsylvania oil man, he had the resources to develop the mines, and also to process the metal in his own smelter he had constructed in the same area. The boom only lasted a short time, however.

As the ore waned and the miners moved out of Galeyville, Curly Bill, John Ringo, and their associates had good reasons to move in. The location was nearby the border with Mexico, where cattle raids were regular. Adjacent gulches were perfect for sorting and altering brands. Galeyville was also close to San Simon, where Curly Bill had a cattle ranch.

As Russian Bill rode through the mountains on his approach to Galeyville, Curly Bill was out in the street conducting a shooting exhibition. A small crowd of men from the saloons and shops on Main Street had gathered to watch. The half-drunk soldier, from among the patrons of the Gem, held a silver half-dollar coin at arm's length. There were cries from Curly Bill to "hold 'er steady" as he aimed his pistol from a twenty-yard distance.

Curly Bill took extra time aiming. He squinted, walked back, stepped forward, changed hands, aimed again, and put the gun down. It was a hot, humid day in the Chiricahua Mountains, and the half-drunk soldier stood very still with sweat dripping down his face. Then, with no warning, Curly Bill pulled the other gun, twirled them both, threw them high in the air, caught them and fired off one shot from each. The first shot hit the coin squarely and sent it flying down the street. The second one hit it again and sent it even further into the Main Street dirt.

The noise attracted the attention of a drunken miner whom everyone in those parts came to know as Staggering Bum. He rushed out of McCarthy's Saloon, saw the coin land, wobbled over to get it, and, with great difficulty, picked it up and carried it back into McCarthy's.

Curly Bill was interested in demonstrating

more trick shots, but the half-drunk soldier said he was thirsty and weak from the heat, and that his arm and shoulder hurt from holding out the coin for so long. The rest of the crowd dispersed and walked back into the numerous Galeyville saloons.

CHAPTER 12

Tombstone sheriff Johnny Behan's deputy, Billy Breakenridge, was in Galeyville on official duty. His assignment was to serve a summons to the owner of the Higbee general store. After performing his duty, he exited the store with his leather satchel, and lit a cigar. Then he watched with interest as Russian Bill rode into town and tied up his white horse in front of McCarthy's saloon across the street.

Breakenridge watched with the hint of a smile on his cigar-puffing lips as Russian Bill walked into McCarthy's, and then quickly exited to a chorus of laughs and shouts. Exhaling a cloud of smoke, he decided to speak to the man in the white, fringed buckskins.

"Hello, you across the street."

Russian Bill looked all around. "You are speaking to me, sir?" Russian Bill kept his hands close to his holsters.

"That's quite an outfit you have on. Didn't I see you in Tombstone the other day?"

Russian Bill began crossing the street slowly, his eyes on Breakenridge with concern for his movements. He sized this man as grossly overweight, a *nepebec* in his language. And wearing spectacles, probably a reader of books like himself.

Russian Bill removed his hat and ran the fingers from his left hand through his hair, keeping his right hand ready for any possible trouble. He carefully replaced the white hat on his head. "I was in Tombstone, yes, but I don't recall meeting into you. But I wonder something. When I checked into hotel there was a man sitting in lobby watching me. Every time I turned to look at him the newspaper would move in front of his face. Maybe you wear glasses to read newspaper in hotel lobby?"

Breakenridge laughed. "That's what it was. That wasn't me. It was my boss, Sheriff Johnny Behan, spying on you from behind that newspaper. I am his deputy, William Breakenridge. Johnny described you as a suspicious character. Told me to be on the lookout for you."

Russian Bill smiled. "You are William? I am William, too. William R. Tettenborn. I am suspicious? Good, good. I like to hear that. Yes, it is true, I am very dangerous man. Killed many in Russia and here. I am very suspicious."

Breakenridge was amused. He puffed on his cigar. "Well, at the risk of my personal safety, may I inquire what you are doing way out here in this godforsaken outlaw camp?"

Russian Bill glanced across the street to make sure that his horse was all right. The horse was tied to the rail with a long enough lead that it was able to turn its head in Russian Bill's direction. Russian Bill was anxious to get it to the stable for some hay and some rest. Then he would continue his search for Curly Bill.

"Of course you may inquire. I am here looking for a Brocius named Curly Bill with which I have something of great importance to discuss. Now, my good deputy, sir, would you be so kind as to advise me of your business in such forsaken outlaw place?"

Breakenridge laughed again. "Well I was sent to serve a summons on the owner of this store. But you helped me make up my mind. I believe if Curly Bill is here, and I have a feeling that he is, well I was thinking about having a few words with him myself."

Russian Bill frowned. "Why you always

laugh at me? Maybe you won't think it's so much funny when bullets fly."

Breakenridge exhaled a puff of smoke. "I think you are a most unusual man."

Russian Bill lit his own cigar. He looked at Johnny Behan's deputy and said, "Unusual is language because St. Petersburg Russia language is very different from language of Galeyville, Arizona. Unusual outfit is because I meet Buffalo Bill Cody, who is William, too, same as you, me and Curly Bill. Lots of Bills in this west. So unusual outfit, yes, is because I go on buffalo hunt with Buffalo Bill and many others. Sioux Indians go, too. We exchange gifts. Lakota Sioux made gift for me this outfit."

"You don't say."

"Yes, I say. Now kindly please excuse me. I come very long ride. Have adventures along way. Must take horse to stable. Then I must continue search for Curly Bill."

CHAPTER 13

At the same time that Russian Bill was making arrangements for his horse to be fed, watered, brushed, and rested at the Galeyville livery, there was much going on in the Gem Saloon. Curly Bill gang member Jim Wallace was playing poker with one of the two drunken freighters, who had been there all day. The other drunken freighter still sat in a corner and continued to alternate between arguing with his pard from a distance and laughing at some joke known only to himself. Jeff Logan stood behind the bar smoking a cigar. The half-drunk soldier sat at a table whittling a piece of wood and making a mess on the table and the floor. The mountain man had left with his dogs. Curly Bill was asleep on one of the table tops, isolated from the other tables.

When Billy Breakenridge entered through the swinging doors, Jim Wallace watched him walk to the bar. Then he threw his cards down. "I smell a badge."

"You smell what?" the freighter asked.

"A badge. Badges make my eyes water, my throat gets tight, and they make me sneeze. And another thing, they make my fingers ball up where the only thing to stop it is to smash somebody in the face."

Wallace contorted his face like he was going to sneeze, but instead of bringing forth a normal sneeze, he sneezed something else. "Ah-horseshit!"

That caused Breakenridge to stare at Wallace for a moment. They locked eyes but no further words were uttered. Breakenridge swung back to Jeff Logan and ordered whiskey. Jeff poured him one, and when Breakenridge picked up the glass to have a drink Wallace started in on him.

"Hey you, chubby. Ain't you Johnny Behan's deputy over in Tombstone? Didn't you lock me up couple months ago for shootin' at the moon?"

Breakenridge cleaned his glasses with a bandana. He downed his drink. Then he turned to Wallace. "You were a very bad shot. There was considerable damage to private property. You might recall that Judge Reilly agreed. You were fined, which in my opinion was generously on the low side considering the damage, and you spent a couple nights in jail. Maybe you think that towns like Tombstone should give out awards for who can do the most damage shooting up the town and terrorizing the citizens. Anyway, as far as I'm concerned you got drunk, you had your fun and you paid for it. All that is over now and . . ."

Wallace interrupted. "It's not over, Breakenridge. It's far from over."

The deputy turned to Jeff Logan and asked if he had seen Curly Bill in there lately.

Jeff Logan head-motioned toward Curly Bill, who was sleeping on a table. Then he remembered something. He lifted his watch from his vest pocket and stared at it a few seconds before carefully replacing it. He grabbed a bucket he had stashed behind the bar, along with a ladle and a towel, and took it over to Curly Bill. He stood by Curly Bill's head and said, "Here's your water, Curly Bill, right on time, just like you told me."

Curly Bill woke up startled and wild-eyed. He said in a groggy voice, "That ain't water, that's piss!" Not fully awake, he shot the ladle out of Jeff Logan's hand. The bullet passed through the Gem's plank side wall. A horse whinnied loudly outside.

That's exactly when Russian Bill entered

the Gem. He announced, "I heard shot, saw horse fall dead around corner."

Jim Wallace stared at the stranger in white buckskins. "Over there is where you keep your horse, ain't it Curly?"

Curly Bill slid off the table and sat in a chair. He put his head in his hands. "Damn it all! Who are these intruders, Jeff?"

Before Jeff Logan could answer, Jim Wallace spoke right up. "I don't know anything about the circus act that just come in, but this here fat fella is Johnny Behan's deputy from Tombstone."

Russian Bill noticed Breakenridge giving Jim Wallace a look of disgust.

"I am William Breakenridge," he said. "I'm in town on official business to serve a summons, which I did a few minutes ago in Higbee's store. Mr. Wallace is correct. I am deputy sheriff under Johnny Behan. I'm sure you are aware that a new county called Cochise has been formed to help the mining towns like Tombstone, Bisbee, and all the way up here to run more efficiently. Well, I've been appointed Tax Assessor for the new county."

Russian Bill stepped forward. "Excuse me, gentlemen. Mr. Curly Bill, sir, I have come a very long way to speak with you. My own horse is in livery. It would be honor if you will allow me to make arrangements for taking care of beloved dead horse and buying new one. Livery can handle arrangements and I will pay. First I would be grateful to have honor to buy for everybody drinks."

Curly Bill stood up and walked over to the bar, not taking his eyes off Russian Bill. "You are one crazy greenhorn coming up here in that getup. Who are you, where did you come from, and why are you tracking me?"

He nodded to Jeff Logan, who filled a glass and pushed it to Curly Bill.

"I am William R. Tettenborn. I come St. Petersburg from Russia, where I was officer in Imperial Guards. My mother, she is royalty. I come to America first in New York. Go all over, meet many dignitaries. In St. Louis I read about outlaws in west. Curly Bill and others. I kill man in my country, other officer. I had good reason but does not make difference. In Russia you kill officer you are outlaw. I get reputation, and other soldiers, other men, they fear me. I enjoy that. Came here to join with Curly Bill and gang of outlaws and rustlers of cows."

Jim Wallace snickered. "Well, if that don't beat everything."

Upon hearing Russian Bill's speech, Billy

Breakenridge said, "You are making a serious mistake, William. These men are ruthless. There's no place in a gang like this for a gentleman."

Curly Bill was quite upset about shooting his own horse, and by having one of his hangouts invaded by incompetent hunters, uninvited lawmen, and whatever it was that Russian Bill represented. He told Billy Breakenridge to shut up so he could think. After a pause he addressed Russian Bill. "What did you say your name was?"

"William R. Tettenborn."

"Not no more it ain't. From now on, goddammit, you'll go by Russian Bill. I mean, look at you. William R. Tettenborn, my ass. You are Russian Bill."

When Russian Bill heard that he got perky and spry. "Russian Bill? Me? Oh, thank you, sir. I very much like this name. Russian Bill." He turned to a small mirror on the opposite wall that Curly Bill accidentally shot his horse through, and looked at his own image. "I am Russian Bill. I am very bad outlaw. Do not get in my way."

Curly Bill was starting to be amused. He said, "Now what was it that you read about me, Russian Bill?"

"That you are king of all outlaws in territory Arizona."

Curly Bill chuckled when he heard that. "You hear that, boys? The king of all outlaws in territory Arizona. Let me tell you something, Russian Bill. What you read is true. Don't tell that deputy over there, but I am the leader of a bunch of fun-loving Texans and other ruffians that are not necessarily ruthless, but just can't resist certain things like picking up a rope that has a horse on the other end, or maybe a cow now and then. Or a herd down in Mexico."

Deputy Breakenridge smiled. "I heard that, Curly Bill."

Curly Bill waved that off. "Out here you can't say things like 'may I have the honor of buying everyone drinks?' If you want to be trusted and accepted, you have to say 'slide on up to the bar, boys, and nominate your pizen.' "

Jim Wallace made sniffing noises with his nose in the air. "Sure is whiffy in here. Smells like sheepherders' socks."

Billy Breakenridge understood that these remarks were intended for his ears. "You got a big mouth, Wallace. You could take a lesson or two in manners from Tettenborn here."

Wallace sniffed in the air again. "That so, Breakenridge? That'll be the day when I take any kind o' lesson from a white Chinaman like this greenhorn who, as far as I'm concerned, is just handing out a lot of Mexican oats. Like how he's a bad-ass outlaw, and he's a cold-blooded killer, and his mother is royalty."

Russian Bill had sat down after looking in the mirror. Now he stood back up. "I don't know what this means, but I understand it is no compliment. May I please have interpretation for understanding if that is insult to my person?" He locked eyes with Jim Wallace. "Are you picking fight with me? William R. Tettenborn allowed no insults to person. Russian Bill will certainly not. Maybe we will have encounter with fisticuffs, see who stands and which falls down."

Breakenridge said, "You're drunk, Wallace. This man Tettenborn hasn't done a thing to warrant your drunken taunts."

Jim Wallace was in a fighting mood. "You've got a lot of nerve, Breakenridge, coming in here and acting all high and mighty after throwing me in that flea-ridden cracker-box jail in Tombstone. Come on, Curly Bill. How come you ain't saying nothing? Why do I have to listen to this sumbitch deputy and this, this son of the Queen of Russia?"

Wallace grabbed a bottle out of the hand of the drunken freighter standing at the bar and took a full swallow. Then he sneezed extra loudly for the benefit of everyone in the room, and anyone who might be passing by outside. "Ah-horseshit!"

Russian Bill forced himself to smile. He looked at Curly Bill. "If this man Wallace is your friend, maybe I will forget these insults. Perhaps I will slide to bar and nominate poison for this man to drink."

Curly Bill's blue eyes twinkled with delight. He smiled back and nodded approval.

Russian Bill walked over to Jim Wallace. He said, "If we are to ride together in Curly Bill's gang, we must make attempt to get along. I am willing to forget what you said and purchase more poison for you."

At that moment Staggering Bum excitedly rushed into the saloon looking for Curly Bill. When he found him, he spoke to him in slurred words, and he shuffled back and forth on his feet.

"Curly Bill, I have important information!"

Curly Bill motioned for Jeff Logan to pour a drink. The bartender did so and he pushed it across the bar. Staggering Bum drank it down and turned to face Curly Bill.

"There's a deputy in town what served some papers to old Higbee at his store. Higbee said he was asking questions about you."

Billy Breakenridge chuckled. "Over here, sir. That would be me."

Staggering Bum grabbed at his heart and lost his balance for a moment. He whispered, "Curly Bill, that deputy's here!"

Curly Bill was more patient with this man than he was with anyone else. "All right, all right. I already know about him. Now get on out of here."

But Staggering Bum was not quite finished. "Wait! I got more information." He looked at Jeff Logan, and Jeff Logan turned to Curly Bill. Curly Bill hesitated but finally waved approval. Another whiskey was poured and slid across the bar.

Curly Bill looked sternly at Staggering Bum. "This better be good."

Staggering Bum removed his filthy, almost shapeless hat and started crying.

Curly Bill said, "Well?"

Staggering Bum had a hard time getting it out. "Somebody shot your hoss!"

Curly Bill threw his arms up in the air. "Now get on outta here, Bum. I know all about that, too."

Staggering Bum wiped his eyes with both hands. "Your hoss is dead!"

Curly Bill stood up. "And your staggering ass is gonna be dead, too, if you don't get the hell outta here!"

Staggering Bum began to rush out of the Gem but paused long enough to give Russian Bill a once-over.

Curly Bill turned to Jeff Logan. "This must be my lucky day. Not only do I shoot my own horse, I've got a Russian greenhorn who wants to join my gang, a deputy asking questions about me and drinking here in my home saloon, a bum who comes in here telling me everything I already know, and a Lincoln County enforcer who's trying to pick a fight with everybody."

Then he turned to the deputy. "All right, Breakenridge, let's get this over with. What do you want with me?"

Billy Breakenridge motioned to Wallace. Then he asked if they might talk privately.

Curly Bill motioned to the table that he had previously napped on. He indicated to Jeff Logan with a few gestures that he wanted a bottle and two glasses brought over. Once they sat down at the table, Curly Bill sat back in a relaxed position.

Breakenridge was sweating. He removed his hat and mopped his head and face with a red bandana. Then he spoke quietly so as not to let any big ears in on his proposition. "I'll get right to the point. As I said before, I have been appointed Tax Assessor for the new county. All enterprises, whether legal or not so legal, will have to pay taxes each year. I can manage fine by myself in Tombstone and Bisbee and some of the other towns. But, Curly Bill, I believe I'd like to hire you as a deputy assessor to help me collect taxes in the southeastern, more rural sections of the county. The deputy assessor will assist me with my collection duties, persuade some of the more reluctant citizens to pay their fair share, and protect me and keep the money I collect safe."

Curly Bill smiled, and there was a noticeable twinkle in his eyes. "Really now? Tell me, Breakenridge, whose idea was this, and why should I do it?"

"The idea was mine alone. I was thinking about it on the ride up here, but didn't know if I would run into you, or have the nerve to speak to you about it if I did. Then I ran into Tettenborn here, and he told me he was gonna speak to you. That made me decide once and for all to at least run it by you. Why should you do it? Well, maybe you'll do it because you think it's your civic duty. Or maybe because of the generous commissions I'll give you on everything you help me collect."

He and Curly Bill downed their drinks. Curly Bill refilled the glasses. Breakenridge leaned in close. "Or maybe you are really smart, and you think it will look good if you ever have to appear before a Cochise County judge. And of course there's always the possibility that, since, as you say, you are a fun-loving Texan, wearing a badge and assisting an officer will be a humorous diversion from your normal routine."

Curly Bill laughed. "A humorous diversion! Yeah, I can just about see some of these boys when I ask them to pay up. All right, Breakenridge, I guess you've got yourself a deputy tax assessor."

He poured more whiskey into their glasses, which they clinked together to commemorate their business arrangement. After downing their drinks, Curly Bill sat up straight. He said in a softer voice, "Now send over that crazy Russian sumbitch. I gotta find a way to get rid of him."

CHAPTER 14

Over at the livery stable Russian Bill was looking over the horses that were for sale. He had been told by Curly Bill that he was not the right fit to join his gang. But Russian Bill was not ready to give up. He was fairly certain that he could win Curly Bill over in the end. He thought that the gift of the right replacement horse might go a long way in that regard.

Money was not yet a concern. It was true that he had been a free-spender when it came to treating friends and strangers, but he had brought a large amount of gold from Russia, which he quickly exchanged for American gold and currency when he had first arrived in New York. All of the dignitaries did the same thing. In fact, it had been arranged through diplomatic circles, so no one in the large party would be cheated by unscrupulous banks and money changers, as so many foreigners were.

The horses he looked at seemed tired and worn. He stopped for a moment to snuggle with his own horse, which he observed was watching him. Then he noticed a pure black mare with clear bright eyes. He walked over and began running his hand along its head and neck, down along the back, down each leg, one at a time, lifting each to check the hooves. When he was satisfied, he turned to the proprietor, a man named Smiley, who had been given that name years ago when it had been determined that he never ever smiled.

"How much do you ask for this mare?"

Smiley frowned. "You have good eyes. I won't take less than sixty for that there beauty."

Russian Bill motioned for Smiley to come closer. He spoke as though what he was about to say was a secret he was letting Smiley in on. "This horse is for Curly Bill himself. He told me real price is half what you say first. So how about deal between gentlemen? I give you forty dollars gold. You give horse and owner papers to Curly Bill. You pick up dead horse. Put saddle and bridle on new horse. Dispose of beloved dead horse with respect. That all okay?"

"You know I'll have to drag . . ."

"No, please don't tell me things like that.

Respect and dignity is what I ask for. I know you love horses or you would not be proprietor of stable. Treat dead horse like you would your own is all I ask for. Don't let coyotes eat."

"Mister, you don't know what you're asking."

"I give you fifty right now. That's a lot of money. You don't accept, that's okay, too. I keep money and tell Curly Bill I tried but could not make deal."

Smiley frowned. "Okay, mister. Fifty will be fine and I'll take care of everything."

CHAPTER 15

In the Gem Saloon Curly Bill and Jim Wallace were in each other's faces.

Curly Bill yelled, "I don't care if he did lock you up. You think I haven't been locked up in Tombstone? I have a business arrangement with him. You had no call to talk him down that way."

"No call? Are you . . ."

Curly Bill interrupted, "And the dude, Russian Bill, what'd he do to you?"

"He's disturbing my peace is what he's done. How can I relax with him in here dressed like an idiot and tellin' tall tales?"

Curly Bill took another drink. "I'm sick of your whining, Wallace. You go and apologize to Breakenridge right now. And when Russian Bill gets back, you apologize to him, too."

Jim Wallace was turning red. "Me apologize? Hell, no. You should be the one apologizing to me for not taking my side against these two."

Curly Bill took another drink. "I've only known you a couple of months. You are a loud-mouth instigator. You can't keep your mouth shut and you pick a fight with everybody when you're drinking. My God, man, give it a break. Now get over there right now and apologize to Deputy Breakenridge."

Jim Wallace breathed deeply. "You really want to do this to me? Well, okay, then."

He calmly walked over to Breakenridge. He stood before him and said, "Deputy Breakenridge, I apologize for insulting you."

Here he paused and looked at Curly Bill, who smiled and nodded approval. He took a drink from the bottle he was still carrying, smiled back at Curly Bill, and turned again to Breakenridge.

"As I was saying, I apologize and I sincerely hope that I didn't hurt your feelings, you fat, four-eyed, piece o'shit sumbitch!"

Before Billy Breakenridge had a chance to prepare, Wallace pushed him violently, knocking him down. Then he quickly exited the Gem, crashing into Russian Bill, who was just coming in.

Curly Bill stood up, throwing his chair backwards. He momentarily lost his balance and grabbed onto the table, yelling after Wallace, "I will kill you, you goddamn Lincoln County sumbitch!"

Billy Breakenridge and Russian Bill approached Curly Bill. Breakenridge said, "That was a clear threat, Bill. Let me borrow your guns for a little while. We'll have Jeff hold them behind the bar for a bit."

"Not a chance!"

Russian Bill found the moment to be right and asked if Curly Bill wanted to see his new horse.

"Yes, I do," Curly Bill answered. "But I want to make sure you understand that what I said before still stands. You are not going to ride with my gang. You are too much of a gentleman to fit in. My boys will laugh at you, like that tomfool Wallace just did, and I can't take the time to step in. My safety and the safety of all my boys depends on my concentrating on whatever job we're doing."

Russian Bill hung his head like someone in his family died. Then he looked up. "Please, Curly Bill, give me chance. I will take care of myself. This means everything to me."

"Look," Curly Bill said. "I appreciate what you did for me with my horse. I like you, Russian Bill. You got some kind of gravel in you. We can be pards, but I'm afraid the answer has to be no."

The two of them, along with Billy Break-enridge, headed for the doors, having no suspicion about the trouble that waited outside.

CHAPTER 16

The three Bills stepped out of the Gem as a group, and as soon as they were standing on the boards, Jim Wallace emerged from behind Curly Bill's new horse. He raised his gun. "Take this, Mr. King of all outlaws!"

Immediately Curly Bill reached for his guns and Russian Bill leaped through the air at Jim Wallace, just as Wallace squeezed off one shot. Russian Bill landed on Wallace and grappled with him. Curly Bill collapsed and clutched his neck and jaw. Billy Breakenridge drew his gun. "Get his gun, William! It's okay, I've got you covered."

The nearby saloons and businesses emptied, and all manner of townfolk gathered in the street. Billy Breakenridge kept his gun trained on Wallace as he kneeled down close to Curly Bill.

Curly Bill saw that his hands were bloody. "Who shot me?"

Breakenridge said, "Jim Wallace. I'm

gonna take him back to Tombstone and lock him up in his favorite flea-trap jail. And I better get him outta here before these people start taking sides. William jumped on him, probably deflected the shot. Most likely he saved your life."

Breakenridge turned to watch Russian Bill get off of Wallace and lift him up. Still keeping his gun on Wallace, Breakenridge said to Curly Bill, "William and I are witnesses. You're gonna need a doctor. We can work out the tax assessing later."

Curly Bill said, damn his jaw and neck hurt, and damn Jim Wallace, and damn, damn, damn!

CHAPTER 17

Russian Bill and Curly Bill rode into Will-cox side by side. Curly Bill had a bloody scarf wrapped tightly around his face and neck. At the home of Dr. James Morse, Russian Bill dismounted and ran up to the front door. Curly Bill remained on his new black mare, his head bowed.

Russian Bill knocked frantically on the front door. "Emergency! Emergency!" he yelled.

Dr. Morse opened the door. "You again," he said.

Russian Bill shuffled around on the porch. "Yes, I have famous man here. Curly Bill Brocius. He is shot through neck into mouth. Extract few teeth out hole in cheek. Has much pain."

Dr. Morse gave instructions to bring the patient inside immediately. Russian Bill asked how Ned Warner was doing.

"He is doing very well. You can see for

yourself inside."

Curly Bill shouted with great difficulty, "I hope you have something strong for the pain, doc."

Dr. Morse told him that he would do his best to make him as comfortable as possible.

A few minutes later, Curly Bill was seated in a large, wooden chair, his head held still with a metal contraption, while Dr. Morse went to work cleaning and stitching the wounds. Ned Warner, looking much better, sat in another chair and jabbered incessantly. Russian Bill sat in yet another chair and was working his comb.

Ned Warner said, "So after the Mezkins left, I just kinda laid there, turning the green grass red. I couldn't walk much and there was nowhere to go out there, so I just closed my eyes. When I woke up there was buzzards circling, and I didn't even have my guns 'cause them thieving Mezkins took 'em along with all the beeves I rounded up. So I'm a-thinking I'm gonna die like any time now, and those buzzards are gonna eat my face. It isn't the dying that scared me, but the buzzards and the coyotes and the red ants. My hatred is partial to red ants. I was thinking that my body would be stripped clean and nobody would find me. It was a lonely way to die, and I made up my mind that I was holding a ticket to just that event.

"So what do I do then you ask? I start praying. Yeah, can you imagine that? And I don't pray for my life to be spared, 'cause there's no way I deserve any of that kind of consideration. I just prayed that the buzzards wouldn't pluck out my eyes, and the coyotes, well ain't no use thinking about what they'd do. So I'm praying real hard, sure that I'm gonna die any second now. Then I look up and here's this stranger."

Ned Warner pointed to Russian Bill.

"I look up and everything is light and airy. The buzzards are gone, and all I see is him, all dressed in white on a big, white horse. In all my years I never seen a horse like that. The rays of the sun, I swear, were filtering down around him. There was no doubt in my mind that he was an angel or a saint. And then how he got me here I'll never know, 'cause I don't remember anything except him telling me in a soft, strange voice that I was not gonna die, but that I had to believe it."

Here he paused and sighed deeply.

"Now I see that he has helped you, Curly Bill, in your hour of need. So I ask you, once and for all, is he an angel or what?"

It was a struggle for Curly Bill to speak,

but he tried anyway. "This stranger is no angel, and no stranger, either. This here mortal man is none other than Russian Bill."

Russian Bill tucked the comb away and put his hat back on. He beamed with pride.

Dr. Morse could not do his work while Curly Bill spoke. "Mr. Brocius, I must insist that you stop trying to speak while I'm applying the stitches."

Curly Bill shifted in the treatment chair. "Tell you what, doc. Give me more laudanum and tell your other patient here, babbling Ned, who's making more noise than my old sow did when she got her tit caught in the gate, to shut up for a while. I'm in a grumpy mood and I wouldn't want anything to interfere with his complete recovery."

Dr. Morse told Ned to please be quiet. Then he started to leave to get the medication.

Ned Warner said, "Oh, I need some, too!"

Doc Morse threw his hands in the air and left the room.

CHAPTER 18

Over the New Mexico border in Shakespeare, a barking, black dog chased a fox through the deserted street. The fox dodged around, then ran up to the front door of the general merchandise store. There it stopped and turned to face the dog, which had also stopped. There was a silent staring contest for a few seconds until the fox bared its teeth and hissed. The dog lowered its stature, yelped, and trotted away. The fox looked around, its head held high. Then it loped away, spooking some of the horses tied to the hitching rail.

Jackson Price exited the Stratford Hotel and crossed the street on a diagonal. He entered the general merchandise store knowing nothing of the drama that had just ended between the fox and the dog. He passed a clerk and a customer on his way to the rear, where he walked down a narrow stairway and entered a smoky downstairs storage room. A dozen men sat in wooden chairs. Several men were engaged in conversation, but everyone became quiet at once when Jackson Price arrived.

As superintendent of the Shakespeare Mining Company, Jackson Price commanded the respect and admiration of everyone in the room. Several men in attendance had been helped in some major or minor way, which they knew was most unusual from the superintendent of the largest and most important employer in town. And everyone in the room knew that the boss was never too busy to talk to them if they had any issues on the job.

Jackson Price looked around the room. "I want to thank each and every one of you for coming. We've talked about doing this for a long time. I'm glad the day has finally arrived when we can get ourselves organized. Before we discuss the issues, we need to elect a captain. I have volunteered to lead you, but I am not opposed to challenges or additional candidates. So please, if any of you would like to be in charge, or if you object to me being in charge, please stand up now and we can take a vote."

Everyone looked around, but no one stood.

"All right. Let me tell you how I see this.

In terms of organization, we need a name and a purpose. This can be discussed and decided right now. We don't need no secretary to write anything down. What we decide today and in the future is between us."

A miner by the name of Robert Hart stood up. "I got an idea for a name. How about we call ourselves the Shakespeare Guards?"

Jackson Price smiled. "Hold on a minute there, Bob. That's a good name and one we should consider, but before we get to that, we need to all be together with a purpose. You are all keenly aware of the Apache raids we suffer from time to time. I don't see any letting up in the near future, so we need to be ready to fight each time we are threatened or attacked.

"As superintendent of the Shakespeare Mining Company, I'm also concerned with the number and increasing boldness of the marauding outlaws that are robbing banks and merchants, holding up coaches and trains, rustling cattle and horses, shooting up towns, and causing other disturbances of the peace. We hear that Tombstone to the west and Silver City to the north are overrun with them lately. However, these towns have local and county officers of the law.

95

Here in Shakespeare we don't yet.

"There are problems on both sides of the Arizona border with murderous results. About three weeks ago Curly Bill Brocius, who we often see here in town, was shot from ambush over in Galeyville. He was seriously wounded but is likely to recover. The would-be assassin, Jim Wallace, who we have also entertained, was arrested by a deputy sheriff and taken before a justice. He was acquitted on grounds of self-defense.

"Maybe if we knew all the facts, which we don't, we would agree with that verdict. Some folks didn't, though, because Jim Wallace's body was found in a manure pile with fourteen holes perforating it. Known outlaws like John Ringo and that wild kid, Jim Hughes, whose father, Nick, owns the butcher shop, have been relatively well-behaved here in Shakespeare, but their reputations indicate that they can suddenly turn the other way."

CHAPTER 19

At the same time the citizens of Shakespeare were organizing their vigilante committee, John Ringo and Jim Hughes rode into Tombstone. They had been away on a big "business" trip with several of the boys, and all of them had been out of touch with the rest of the gang. They had not heard about Curly Bill, and were just starting to track him.

In the lobby of the Cosmopolitan Hotel, Ringo spotted a man reading a newspaper. He and Jim Hughes approached.

"That you, Johnny?" Ringo inquired.

Sheriff Behan put down the newspaper. "Well, well, Mr. Ringo and Mr. Hughes. What brings you gents to Tombstone this fine day?"

It was not a well-kept secret that Sheriff Behan had a cordial, or even cooperative, relationship with Curly Bill, John Ringo, the Clantons and other cowboys of questionable reputation. So, the fact that the sheriff was having a conference with Curly Bill's right-hand man in a public place probably would not have surprised anyone who might have heard their conversation.

Ringo said quietly, "We were wondering if you've seen Curly Bill lately?"

Sheriff Behan was surprised to hear that from Ringo. "Where have you been? He was shot about three weeks ago. Shot through the neck and jaw over in Galeyville."

Ringo and Jim Hughes tensed up and looked at each other.

Ringo removed his hat and brushed some hair out of his eyes. "We were away on business. So, what the hell happened?"

Behan related how his deputy, Billy Breakenridge, happened to be in Galeyville on official business, and had been present at the scene when the shooting occurred. Then Behan asked if they had heard about the unusual stranger who had been poking around, making bold claims and asking questions about Curly Bill. And Behan said that that very stranger had been right there in the Cosmopolitan Hotel only a few days before the shooting.

Suddenly Jim Hughes remembered something. "Say, Johnny, what did this stranger look like?"

"He had long, yellow hair and was dressed in white buckskins, like Buffalo Bill."

Jim Hughes shouted, "Him! I ran into that dude on the trail. He actually tried to pull that horse trading scheme on me. Can you imagine that? But I got the best of him you can bet and sent him on his way."

Ringo gave his young friend a questioning look, and then asked Sheriff Behan if this yellow-haired stranger was the one who shot Curly Bill.

"I thought he looked mighty suspicious when I saw him in here, but it turns out, according to Break, my deputy, that stranger probably saved Curly Bill's life by jumping on Jim Wallace at the same time he was pulling the trigger."

Ringo's jaw dropped. "Jim Wallace?"

Behan nodded. "Yeah, he's the one that shot Curly Bill."

Jim Hughes said, "Jim Wallace, no!"

Ringo asked if Jim Wallace was in jail, because he would like a word or two with him.

" 'Fraid that won't happen," Behan said. "He was shot fourteen times and dumped in a pile of horse shit."

"And what is his name, this stranger with the long, yellow hair, the one who saved Curly Bill's life?"

"Well, his name is William Tettenborn, but Curly Bill changed it. He's from Russia. Now he goes by Russian Bill."

Chapter 20

For almost a month Russian Bill had been taking care of Curly Bill in a Willcox boarding house room. The room had a bed, a dresser, throw rugs on the floor, curtains drawn shut on the window, and two wooden chairs. Russian Bill had a room just like it directly across the hall, but he spent most of his time in Curly Bill's room, keeping him occupied by telling him his life's story, reading to him and attending to Curly Bill's recovery in every way possible.

Curly Bill was propped up in bed with a bowl of soup on a tray.

Russian Bill poured himself a glass of whiskey and downed it in one noiseless gulp. He said, "Finish your soup and you can have whiskey."

Curly Bill set aside the tray. "I don't want any more soup. I'm sick of soup. Besides, it's cold. It's been almost a month since I had any real food. And I want to get out of here. I need to get outdoors where I can breathe fresh air and see the stars at night, and maybe have a little fun."

Russian Bill started to remind him of some of Dr. Morse's instructions, but it was no use. Curly Bill's mind was made up.

"The hell with Dr. Morse," Curly Bill said with a scowl. "Gimme that bottle. I'm riding out of here tomorrow morning."

Russian Bill took the tray from the bed and placed it on the dresser. He handed over the bottle. Then he spoke in a soft voice. "I see your mind is made up. I think you can get by if you slowly move into activities and not push too hard."

He sat down and continued. "You have known me now for many days and weeks. You can see I am sincerely wanting to join with you and be member of your gang. Will you now put aside any doubts you have of my ability to be of great benefit to you and your men, and allow me extreme privilege of accompanying you on your continued journey?"

Curly Bill took another drink. "No, and here's why. You are too much of a gentleman and are too polite. I don't think you can help yourself, and I don't think you can change. How many times do I have to tell you to stop talking about being sincere, and how extreme a privilege everything is? My God, man, is it an extreme privilege to wipe your ass in the outhouse?"

He poured himself another drink and passed the bottle. Then he watched Russian Bill pour into his own glass, but only fill it up halfway.

Curly Bill touched the scar on his neck. "Don't ever do that again."

Russian Bill was confused. "What I do?"

"Look, I think you saved my life back there in Galeyville, and you've been caring for me real good, so I'm gonna teach you a few things about how we do things out here. First and foremost, always fill your whiskey glass to the brim."

Russian Bill looked at the half-filled glass in his hand and smiled. "All right."

"Don't ever order anything weaker than whiskey."

"I won't."

Curly Bill paused to consider how far to take this discussion. He decided to keep it going. "Here's another thing. Always pick up your whiskey glass with your gun hand to show you have friendly intentions. Of course that's off if you're drinking with Wyatt Earp or any of his goddamn brothers, or that coughing dentist, Doc Holliday.

Don't ever show that lot any courtesy at all."

"I will remember those names."

Curly Bill got up to look at his scars in the mirror. "Here's a few rules about horses. Don't wave at a man on a horse. It might spook the horse. A nod is the proper greeting."

"Okay."

"No matter how tired or hungry or drunk or pissed off you are after a long ride, always see to your horse's needs before your own."

Russian Bill smiled. "I always do that."

"And this is the most important rule because it can cost you your life. Don't ever ride another man's horse without his permission. Even touching another man's horse is almost as bad as touching his wife. Always remember that out here a horse thief pays with his life."

Russian Bill thought deeply about that as he poured whiskey into his glass all the way to the brim.

CHAPTER 21

The two Bills stood on the sidewalk on Railroad Avenue watching a group of wranglers unload several boxcars of cattle from a Southern Pacific Railroad train. A heavy smell of cattle hung in the sultry summer air, and the various bovine moos and cowboy whistles assaulted the unusually quiet surroundings. Curly Bill, who wore a colorful scarf around his neck and jaw, enjoyed the sights, sounds and smells after being shut in for so long.

Most of the wranglers were busy keeping cattle in line, but a few of them glanced over at Russian Bill in his white buckskins and wondered what a dude dressed like that could possibly be doing in a rough and tumble cattle town like Willcox.

Curly Bill nudged Russian Bill with his elbow. He indicated the cattle being herded into pens adjacent to the train station. "That's my bread and butter."

Russian Bill nodded. "I understand what you say. Please give me a chance to prove myself to you. Is no good that I jump on Jim Wallace, maybe help you that time in Galeyville?"

"I appreciate what you did, Bill. But there is no doubt in my mind that any of my boys, if they were in your boots back there, would have shot that sumbitch. Maybe I wouldn't have had to eat soup all this time, and disappoint all kind of ladies over a wide area. Tell you what, though. To be fair with you, I believe I will give you a chance to prove yourself. Matter of fact, I'll give you five chances to show me something."

Russian Bill smiled and relaxed his body. "That is most fair. Thank you for chances. If I cannot stand up, I will be riding away from here and stop being pest to you."

Ned Warner exited a saloon, noticed the two Bills standing together, and walked over. He tossed the remainder of his cigar into the street and spat.

Curly Bill adjusted his scarf. "Morning, Ned. We're going to have a little fun. See if Russian Bill has the high qualities it takes to become a working associate of ours."

Ned Warner chuckled and rubbed his hands together.

"Him, us? That's agreeable to me and it

sounds like too much fun."

Suddenly a steer broke loose from the others and began running down the street. One of the wranglers calmly threw a rope around its neck and pulled back, rodeo style. But the steer was under a full head of steam, and the wrangler could get no traction in the dirt, so he was drug a long distance, to the delight of the other wranglers, who whistled, jeered, and laughed at their companion. Finally the steer just stopped, and the wrangler led it back to the others without showing any anger toward the frightened animal.

Curly Bill said, "Ned, why don't you snoop around and see if you can find out where them beeves are going? Russian Bill and I are going to get our horses."

CHAPTER 22

Over in Juan Soto's store, the first of five chances was underway. Curly Bill was giving a demonstration of the requirements, as he effortlessly glided to the tobacco counter. Russian Bill and Ned Warner took positions pretending to examine picks and shovels. Although they were pretending to discuss the merits and deficiencies of the various tools, they were watching Curly Bill.

Curly Bill slipped around back of the tobacco counter while Juan Soto was trying to sell a woman some fabric. Curly Bill removed a cigar from the box within the display case, ran it under his nose, and placed it in his shirt pocket with an extra pat. Then he slipped back in front of the counter.

Juan Soto noticed the three men come in, but the woman he was helping was one of his regular customers, and he had built a good business by providing the highest level of personal service. He would see to the needs of the three men as soon as his current customer was satisfied.

Juan Soto turned the bolt of fabric three times, allowing a yard to spread on the desk. "This pretty print came all the way from Boston. It will make nice curtains or a pretty bonnet or two." He smiled. "By the way, did you hear all the talk of the rich new vein of gold they discovered at the 1500-foot level in the Isabella mine in Dos Cabezas?"

Curly Bill chose his moment and again seamlessly slipped behind the counter. This time he abducted two cigars, holding them up for his friends to see before depositing them in the pocket of his blue shirt. He stepped around to the front of the counter just as Juan Soto looked his way.

Juan Soto noticed some movement and figured that the man at the tobacco counter was getting restless. The tall joker in the Buffalo Bill outfit and the other cowboy playing with the shovels would have to wait. His customer was studying the fabric on the bolt. Juan looked in Curly Bill's direction. "I'll be right with you, sir."

Curly Bill smiled. "Take your time."

Juan Soto grabbed a new bolt of fabric and turned back to his customer.

The woman finally made a decision and placed her order for two yards of the new fabric and three yards of the original one, plus some coffee, flour, and sugar. As the provisions were gathered, Curly Bill, Russian Bill and Ned Warner slipped out of the store.

Up Railroad Avenue the three men walked past Foxey's Saloon on the corner and stopped in front of the Norton-Morgan Commercial Company store. Here Curly Bill adjusted his scarf, which had shifted down off his face. He then fished out two of the three cigars from his pocket and passed one of them to Ned. He and Ned each immediately puffed up a good light, and they watched Russian Bill straighten his hat and walk into the store.

His mission, and his first opportunity to impress, was to imitate Curly Bill's previous actions.

It was dark inside the store, having just come in from bright, morning glare. Russian Bill immediately crashed into a fruit stand, knocking down a bushel basket of oranges, spilling them onto the floor. He tried to pick up a few of them, but nervously fumbled before getting them in the basket.

Mr. Norton observed this. "Sir, sir, please, sir. I'll take care of this. Please don't concern yourself."

Russian Bill tipped his hat and took a deep breath. He cautiously moved to the counter as Mr. Norton was busy picking up oranges. There was an open cigar box only a few feet away. He glided toward that box just as he had watched Curly Bill do in the other store. He reached into the box, but before he could remove his hand and lift the cigars it was clutching, he was jolted by the loud meow of a cat at his feet. It frightened him so badly that he knocked the open box over the counter to the floor on the other side.

Mr. Norton was still picking up oranges, some of which had rolled to different areas, but he had observed this new disturbance. "I'll be right there, sir."

Peeking over the counter Russian Bill saw Mr. Norton coming his way. That was enough for him to immediately take one step toward the door. That step proved disastrous, though, as he inadvertently stepped on the cat's tail.

The cat, a large, all-black male, which was hanging around for a scratch or a rub, didn't take kindly to having its tail stepped on, and it screamed and hissed and jumped onto a display of soap, knocking it all down and making a huge mess.

Russian Bill was shaken, and he began to

leave. On his way out he said, "I am sorry for trouble, sir. I am afraid I am nervous and excited. I have invested in the Isabella Mine in Dos Cabezas. A large vein of gold was just hit at 1500 feet. I will later come back."

Mr. Norton stood up straight. "Please do. We would be happy to set up credit for you."

Out on Railroad Avenue Russian Bill approached Curly Bill and Ned Warner, who were watching the cattle across the street and puffing on their cigars.

Curly Bill smiled. "Well?" he asked.

Russian Bill bowed his head and said nothing. He reached deep into the front of his pants. Not his pockets, but deep inside his pants.

"What in the hell are you gonna pull out o' there?" Curly Bill asked.

Russian Bill extracted an orange and he held it out. Curly Bill smiled but shook his head.

Ned Warner also smiled, but he nodded yes. Russian Bill tossed him the orange.

CHAPTER 23

Curly Bill wanted some real food, so they all had an early lunch in the A Powers Hotel and Restaurant. Still having jaw pain, Curly spoke to the waiter and, after receiving his assurance that the beef was tender, he placed his order for beef tips over noodles in a dark gravy. Ned Warner thought that sounded fine so he duplicated that order. Russian Bill asked if the cook could make a stroganoff, which he had only had twice since leaving Russia. The waiter checked and returned with a yes and a smile. Seems the cook was from Austria and knew many European dishes. It would be easy for him to adapt the beef tips to a stroganoff, and he was happy to do it.

Next there was a stop at the local gun shop for ammunition and a quick trip to the livery for a handful of horseshoe nails. Curly Bill knew the proprietor of the gun shop, an old Texan named Reese Watley, and chatted with him about the attempt on his life, the extent of his injuries and the details of his recovery. He introduced Russian Bill and Ned Warner. Russian Bill noticed Watley looking at him and he concluded that Curly Bill's friend was just dying to ask questions about him. Those questions would remain unanswered on this day, however, as there was another opportunity at hand for Russian Bill to prove himself worthy.

Curly Bill knew a suitable spot on a nearby ranch. The grass was green and nearly knee-high there. Once they had arrived, Curly Bill affixed three aces to a tree trunk with the horseshoe nails he had in his shirt pocket. From his holster he first drew the right-hand gun. With that he shot the center out of the first two cards. He replayed the draw with his left hand, and from the hip he blasted through the center of the third card. He looked at Russian Bill and Ned Warner with satisfaction as he collected the mangled cards. Then he replaced them with three new aces. He stepped back and nodded to Russian Bill.

Russian Bill drew his right gun quickly, but then slowly lined up the sight to his squinting eye before firing. The shot nicked the upper-left corner of the first card. He pulled the other gun and similarly lined up the shot. This time he clipped the lower-right corner of the second card. He took a deep breath, pulled both guns, and fired from the hip. He hit no cards, but killed a squirrel, which fell from the tree.

CHAPTER 24

Inside Foxey's Saloon back in Willcox, right around the corner from Dr. Morse's residence and across the street from the train station, a poker game was in progress. Curly Bill and Russian Bill sat with a cowboy, a banker, and a miner. The cowboy had just dealt a hand. The banker threw down two cards. "I'll take two," he said, blowing cigar smoke in Russian Bill's direction.

Russian Bill scowled. He pulled a new cigar out of his fringed shirt pocket. "I have my own cigar," he said. "I have no need for yours."

"All right, all right, Wild Bill, take it easy."

"Why you call me Wild Bill? Some people they call me Buffalo Bill, but I am really Russian Bill. Do you understand? Nobody ever calls me Wild Bill."

The banker answered by blowing smoke in the opposite direction and making a waving-off motion to Russian Bill.

The cowboy dealt him two fresh cards. He looked at the miner. "Your bet."

The miner peeked at his cards without changing his expression. "Dollar," he said, tossing chips on the table.

The cowboy raised two.

Russian Bill folded, throwing his cards on the table.

Curly Bill smoothly slipped a card from up his sleeve into his hand, and in another undetectable motion the unwanted card disappeared. "Raise you five," he said smiling.

The cowboy checked his cards and peered into Curly Bill's face. "I think you're bluffing, mister. Your five plus five more."

The miner folded but the banker raised. "His five, your five, and, uh, seven more."

Curly Bill called and laid down his cards. Three aces, with the ace of diamonds on top, were accompanied by a ten and a seven.

The banker angrily threw down his cards. "Damn it all, I have three kings!"

Russian Bill stood up and said, "Thank you, gentlemen. I will now take my leave."

The miner chuckled and said to no one in particular, "He shore do talk funny."

Curly Bill gathered his winnings in his hat and headed to the bar.

CHAPTER 25

Over at the Fashion Saloon another poker game was under way. Russian Bill sat at a table with a merchant, a railroad man, and a ranch hand. The railroad man had just dealt the fifth card. Russian Bill had a hand he liked. He began maneuvering his arm so as to work loose the extra card from up his sleeve.

The ranch hand said, "I'll risk five, boys."

The merchant folded, but Russian Bill raised ten. He was still having trouble shaking the ace of diamonds loose, even though he was twitching and shaking.

The ranch hand noticed his strange movements and said, "Something wrong with you, Buffalo Bill?"

Russian Bill tried to think as he spoke. "Yes, Buffalo Bill, that's a good one, sir. I met him one time, but that is very long story. Maybe I tell you some time. Meanwhile you can call me Russian Bill. Right now I am very itchy. I sleep in hotel last night. I think fleas eat at me."

He stood up and shook and twitched and scratched, all in an effort to get the stuck card out of his sleeve.

The ranch hand laughed. "I'd rather have greybacks than fleas any time. I mean cooties. They graze an' bed down, but a flea ain't never satisfied."

The merchant started scratching. "I'm not even in this hand anymore, and y'all are making me nervous."

"Play cards!" yelled the railroad man. "I'm in this game. Raise ten."

The ranch hand and Russian Bill tossed chips onto the table. Russian Bill shook and twitched one more time to no avail. He thought it was an awkward time to fold, so he called.

Then the ranch hand called.

The railroad man turned over his cards. "Jacks over sevens."

Russian Bill stood up. "Only pair of aces."

"Three fives," said the now-smiling ranch hand. He displayed his cards and swept up the pot.

Russian Bill said, "That's enough for me. I can't sit still. Thank you, gentlemen." He walked to the swinging doors and left the Fashion Saloon.

CHAPTER 26

Out on Railroad Avenue Russian Bill found Curly Bill speaking with two men. He approached them.

Curly Bill saw him coming and shouted, "How'd you make out, Russian Bill?"

Russian Bill lowered his head. "I have to be honest."

Curly Bill stamped his foot on the boards and grabbed at his jaw. "Damn man, you're making me hurt myself. You don't have to be honest. That's the whole point of these exercises."

"Okay, then I win big pot." He glanced over at Curly Bill's companions and recognized the young one. "Hey, I remember you," he said.

He pointed to Jim Hughes and, as he lowered his arm, three aces fell to the ground. "All right, I lose. Sorry I lied. May I please meet your friends?"

Curly Bill was frustrated, but did not want

to jar his jaw again. "Never say you're sorry!" He paused to glare at Russian Bill before continuing. "This here is John Ringo. And the kid is Jim Hughes. They are business associates. Boys, I'd like you to meet Russian Bill."

John Ringo and Jim Hughes looked at Russian Bill but didn't say anything. Jim Hughes shuffled his feet nervously.

Russian Bill smiled. "Naturally I have heard of you, Mr. Ringo. You have exquisite bad reputation. It is honor, sir."

Ringo laughed.

Then Russian Bill glanced over at Jim Hughes. "And you," he said. "Yes, I remember we pass on the trail. I nodded to you for to not possibly spook your horse. You make compliment of my horse. Nice to see you again."

Curly Bill said, "When you meet someone like Ringo, don't say it is an honor, and don't call him sir. And don't speak of his reputation in public. The wrong ears might get the right impression."

"But I am excited to meet this man. What should I say?"

Curly Bill said, "Just say howdy. Now look, Bill. My associates here tell me of a business opportunity that just came up. Time is of the essence. You can accompany us if you like, but we're leaving right now to the border, and it might be dangerous."

Russian Bill smiled. "I fear no danger."

"Then ride with us and pay attention. Your fourth opportunity will come soon. It will be similar to what we will now do but on a much smaller, one-man scale. You have not done well so far, so pay close attention."

Russian Bill happily laughed. "May I please inquire nature of current opportunity?"

Curly Bill answered in one word. "Beef."

CHAPTER 27

Curly Bill, John Ringo, Jim Hughes and Russian Bill rode to the international border. When they arrived there, they found four vaqueros on the Mexican side guarding a sizeable herd of cattle. Curly Bill removed a rifle from its scabbard and fired at the closest Mexican, knocking him off his horse. The other Mexicans returned fire and then hastily retreated.

The cattle mooed and squirmed but did not scatter. Curly Bill and the boys slipped across the border and began driving the herd into Arizona. That's when a shot rang out from the cover of a boulder, knocking off Russian Bill's hat.

Russian Bill yelled, *"Govno,"* as he leaped off his big, white horse to pick up his hat, disgusted that there was now a hole in it.

Curly Bill, Ringo, and Jim Hughes fired rapidly, forcing the Mexicans to scatter into the foothills. As the herd moved fully into

Arizona, Curly Bill and Ringo guarded the border. The herd moved along slowly but steadily. Russian Bill rode happily on one side. Jim Hughes rode up. "I wanted to say thanks for not telling Curly Bill and Ringo what I done. You could have made it dicey for me."

Russian Bill smiled at him. "That's okay, Jim. I know you were only having fun with a stranger."

"Well Jim Hughes don't forget a favor. I owe you one." After saying this, the young outlaw reined his horse to the other side of the herd.

The next afternoon, as the last of the cattle were herded into a large corral, Curly Bill rode up to Russian Bill for a chat.

Russian Bill removed his hat and stuck his finger through the hole, smiling. "How I do?"

Curly Bill smiled. "Fair. You didn't run when the shooting started, but you put yourself in the line of fire when you went for your hat. If you had been shot, we could've left you there for the Mezkins, or made targets out of all our asses trying to retrieve yours. Hats can be replaced." Having said this he turned away and rode toward the big corral.

Russian Bill thought for a minute. Then

he said to no one in particular, "But I really like this hat."

CHAPTER 28

Russian Bill's fourth opportunity to prove himself was to find and relocate a small herd of cattle. After a few hours in the saddle, he came upon six cows grazing in a fenced-in field of high grass. The cows were guarded by a large German Sheperd dog. Russian Bill dismounted, stretched, and carefully looked around.

The dog stood up but had not barked. Russian Bill studied it. "You are dog I think from Germany, but also big ones like you are in Russia. Maybe you were brought to this American west. Are you from motherland? *Vy menya panim Ayete?* Or maybe they bring you from Germany? *Verstehst du?*"

The dog immediately barked and snapped to attention. Russian Bill cut the bob wire between two posts. He looked back at the dog. *"Bitte folgen Sie mir. Bringst die Rinder."*

The dog continued barking and began

rounding up the cows. Russian Bill checked both his guns and his rifle in case the noise should alert any ranchers. Soon, with the cooperation of the dog, which seemed eager to exhibit advanced herding skills, Russian Bill was leading the cows north toward the waiting pens at the San Simon ranch.

He led the cows over a low rolling hill and muttered out loud, "Finally something goes good for me. For once I will impress Curly Bill. When cows get to ranch, I will get dog special bone. Then I will keep dog to assist with outlaw activities."

Time went by and Russian Bill was thinking about his home in Russia. Mostly he thought of the luxury of a soft bed every night. And naturally he thought of his mother, who had spoiled him and given him everything he ever wanted. She had helped him escape to the United States of America when he got himself into serious trouble with a superior officer in the Russian Imperial Guard. He thought about the father he never knew and wondered if the stories his mother told about his gallantry were true and if he had really died in battle at the end of the Crimean War.

He had ridden steadily for quite some time absorbed in thoughts and reminiscences, when the range became so dry it couldn't support a horned toad. A deep feeling of doom washed over him, causing him to shiver. He stopped and looked back and realized that his instincts were true.

The cows and the dog were gone.

"What is this?" he said out loud.

He rode to the top of the hill he had just crossed hoping that the cows were merely lagging behind. That was not the case, however. They were gone.

"Do I lose mind, or is it dog who does this? I tell you this, there will be no special bone for you, *Schwein Hund*!"

CHAPTER 29

The eastbound passenger train pulled into the little station at Bowie, not too many miles from the San Simon ranch with the freshly rebranded cattle. Steam was hissing in the hot Arizona air as the engineer jumped down from the locomotive with an oil can. After adjusting his suspenders he immediately became so involved with oiling some locomotive parts that he did not notice Curly Bill, John Ringo, Jim Hughes and Russian Bill walk up behind him.

When Curly Bill tapped him on the back, it startled him so badly he almost used the outhouse without the benefit of being in an enclosed structure.

The engineer turned away from the locomotive. "Oh, mister, you s'prised me there. What — what can I do for you boys?"

Curly Bill adjusted his scarf. "Do you want to sell this thing?" he said, indicating the locomotive with a sweep of his hand.

Then he smiled.

The engineer thought this was a joke. "That's a good one, mister." He went back and busied himself with more oiling as steam continued to hiss white smoke from the chimney.

Curly Bill spoke louder. "I said, do you want to sell this here locomotive?"

The engineer turned around and smiled, but otherwise ignored the question.

While Ringo, Hughes, and Russian Bill stood back and watched, Curly Bill pulled his gun and shoved it into the engineer's stomach. "I asked you a polite question and I expect a polite answer."

The engineer dropped the oil can and threw his hands high in the air. "I can't sell it to you, mister. It don't b'long to me, honest."

Curly Bill holstered his gun. "Well then, I b'lieve we'll just borrow it for a while."

The engineer froze, his hands still reaching for invisible birds' nests, as Curly Bill, John Ringo, and Russian Bill climbed up onto the locomotive. Jim Hughes cut the engine from the rest of the train, and then he, too, climbed aboard.

Shortly the locomotive began moving slowly down the track. The engineer, astonished, finally lowered his hands, threw off his gloves, rubbed his eyes and watched the locomotive move away. After a few seconds he regained his composure and ran into the station.

He yelled, "The train is robbed! The train is robbed!"

A ticket clerk, a passenger and a large sleeping dog were the only ones inside the small station. The dog raised and lowered an eyelid but otherwise did not budge. The ticket clerk and the passenger both perked up.

"Did they blow the safe?" asked the ticket clerk.

"Did they rob the mail?" asked the passenger.

"Did anyone get hurt?" asked the ticket clerk.

Suddenly the train whistle blew one long and three very short blasts. The men in the station stopped talking and ran outside. The sleeping dog again raised an eyelid, then lowered it and fell back to sleep.

Dozens of passengers stepped quickly off the various now stationary train cars to learn why the train was whistling way up the tracks and why they were apparently stuck at the station in the middle of nowhere. And, above all, why were the railroad people standing around doing nothing while all this was happening?

Up yonder the locomotive appeared to be stopping. Then it started moving again, but this time, after Curly Bill had sufficiently experimented with the levers, it slowly backed to the station.

The engineer and the ticket clerk stood at the front of the stranded train cars and watched as the locomotive returned about halfway to the station. Once again it stopped. The whistle blew a series of long and short blasts. Then it pulled forward again, away from the frustrated railroad workers and passengers.

The engineer turned to the ticket clerk. "Wire Lordsburg and Willcox. Tell them what's happening here and see if they'll send the law! This is ridiculous!"

The ticket clerk hurried back to the station. In the distance the locomotive stopped again, and the whistle blasted two long shrieks. The locomotive backed up slowly to the station. When it arrived, it stopped appropriately up against the other cars.

Russian Bill, Jim Hughes, John Ringo, and Curly Bill swung down from the cab. They walked casually to their horses. The bewildered passengers watched as the four men galloped away toward the not-too-distant mountains.

CHAPTER 30

On a moving train, Russian Bill sat with the other passengers reading a dime novel, of the same western adventure type he had enjoyed during his stay in St. Louis. Every time he looked up he saw a different woman looking his way, smiling at him. Each time, he tipped his hat, smiled, and fussed with his yellow curls. This was one time when he preferred not to be noticed, but he knew it was too late for that now.

The train robbers blew the safe, in the book he was reading, but they had used too much dynamite. The explosion not only tore apart the mail car, but scattered Mexican silver dollars flew like shrapnel into telegraph poles or into the desert sands. United States mail rained down like flat snowflakes or sailed away in wind currents. Russian Bill closed the book and looked up.

This time a man in a derby hat was smiling at him.

Russian Bill quickly removed his watch and studied it. Satisfied that the time was right, he stood up and moved to the front of the car. Even though he noticed that nearly every passenger was watching him, he still exited the train car. In front of him was the coal car, which, in turn, was directly behind the locomotive. Black smoke and soot were flying back at him and, mixed with the hot desert air, made him feel like he was being choked.

There was also the prospect of getting his white buckskins filthy dirty, not only from the thick black particles in the air, but also on the grimy coal car itself. Russian Bill understood that was the price he would have to pay for the final opportunity to impress Curly Bill. All other attempts had been dismal failures. Russian Bill knew well that five opportunities should have produced at least two or three positive impressions of his abilities.

He took a deep breath and began climbing along the coal car, his feet reaching for footholds, and his hands grabbing onto every possible edge. He tried to maintain his balance on the swaying train as it lumbered clackety-clack down the tracks. He also worked at keeping his clothing as far away as possible from the greasy, black, metal car.

As the train continued along the tracks, Russian Bill inched forward, thinking only of the success that would surely come in the next few minutes.

When he reached the end of the coal car, he was able to swing himself up onto the locomotive. The fireman was busy shoveling coal into the furnace and was so startled when a gun was roughly thrust against his back that he jumped and spun around, the shovel he was holding accidentally striking Russian Bill in the head, knocking him completely off the locomotive.

CHAPTER 31

It was just about dusk in Galeyville. Summer rain clouds were rolling in from Mexico and developing overhead, providing a welcome shade over Main Street. Curly Bill, John Ringo, and Jim Hughes sat on their horses in the middle of the thoroughfare. Russian Bill rounded a corner, saw their position and rode up to face them.

Curly Bill wasted no time. "You've got to face facts, Bill. In a few minutes us three are gonna ride off without you. You are not cut out for outlaw life. That should be clear to you by now. None of us think it's your fault. You tried it on for size and it just didn't fit, that's all. I want to thank you for saving my life and for being a good nurse. And also for buying me this horse. She's a good one. You know I was gonna cut you loose before I was shot, but I gave you five chances to show me something. As far as I'm concerned that evens the score. My best advice to you is to find a new career. Good luck and adios."

The three tipped their hats, turned their horses around and rode off, leaving Russian Bill alone.

Russian Bill hung his head. He knew Curly Bill was right, and given the ratio of zero successes to five failures, he was surprised that Curly hadn't cut him off sooner. In Russian he thought, "Probably I am amusement for the outlaws. Maybe they make bets on my failures." The rest of his thoughts were also in Russian as the big, white horse walked him out of Galeyville. "I will now ride to Shakespeare mining town over New Mexico border. Not too far from here. Town named for greatest poet can't be bad place. They don't know me there. Maybe I can keep mouth shut and not be so much fool."

CHAPTER 32

Before Russian Bill reached Shakespeare, Curly Bill separated from Ringo and Hughes. He met up with Pony Diehl, Sherm McMasters, and A. T. Hanbrough at a ranch in the Chiricahuas that was friendly to the cowboys. It was unwritten but understood that providing hospitality to the Curly Bill gang meant protection for your cattle and other resources, including threats against your person. At this ranch, meals and whiskey were provided, and the owners and hands were treated to a night of wild stories and good-natured fun.

Ringo and Hughes had continued on to Charleston and Tombstone where they were to find markets for their most recently re-branded cattle. It was Curly Bill's objective to act quickly when taking appropriated cattle to market.

The next morning Curly Bill and his associates, Diehl, McMasters and Hanbrough, rode by the corrals at Fort John Rucker, and then stopped to pass a whiskey bottle around.

The camp had initially been called Camp Supply, and had been commissioned to protect settlers from marauding Apaches. It was a supply post and also housed a cavalry unit. When Lieutenant John Rucker drowned while trying to save another soldier who had fallen into a storm-swollen river, the camp had been renamed in his honor.

As Curly Bill passed the bottle over to Pony Diehl he noticed six mules grazing just inside the unlocked corral gate, being guarded by a detachment of nobody. "Boys," he said, "do you see what I see?"

The answers were three smiles.

Before the sun went down, the army mules were munching alfalfa on the ranch owned by Frank and Tom McLaury near the Mexican border.

Russian Bill had the romanticized notion that Shakespeare would be a bustling mining town, like Tombstone, with all the sounds of laughter coming from the saloons, the smell of horse manure in the streets, and active people everywhere. But when he first rode into town, there were two businessmen standing outside the assay office and two horses in front of a saloon called Roxy Jay. There was no noise except for the buzz of a fly that, no matter how many times Russian Bill waved it away, kept rebounding to his ear.

There were two hotels in Shakespeare. Russian Bill looked them over from the street and chose the Stratford, an eight-room, one-and-a-half-story, elegant lodging house. He tied his horse to the rail and took a few steps to walk off the saddle stiffness from his back and legs. He looked up and down Avon Street but found no additional activity.

Inside the Stratford House lobby, Russian Bill was surprised with several overstuffed chairs, rich wood tables, Persian rugs, oil paintings in gilt frames on the wall with polished brass sconces spaced at regular intervals. It was tasteful and chic, unlike the Cosmopolitan in Tombstone, which was several cuts above the norm, but shabby in comparison to the Stratford. This reminded him of his home in St. Petersburg, and it made him smile.

He stepped up to the registration counter. The clerk was not present, but two young men, Ross Woods and Bean Belly Smith, were arguing off to the side. A very pretty young lady, Jessie Woods, with long, brown hair, was cleaning. While Russian Bill waited for someone to approach, he alternated his attention between the pretty girl and the two men arguing. One time he looked at the girl's flowing hair and found her staring at him, but she shyly looked back to her chores when their eyes met.

Maybe she is another who considers me a fool because of how I appear, Russian Bill thought. *She has probably lived in this place all her life and has never seen anything like me. She probably is already married or has many suitors. If she would only smile at me . . .*

In the argument, Bean Belly said, "I don't care that your ma owns this hotel. Makes no difference. I'm telling you, Ross Woods, for the last time I had no knowledge that silver mine was a bust. You can just settle down and stop talking shit about me all around town."

Ross Woods's ma did own the Stratford House. Ross stepped close to Bean Belly and said, "Look you. If you want me to stop talking, all you have to do is make the deal right. That mining interest you sold me as a prime investment was sour from the git-go, and you and everybody else know it. You can say anything you want, but that's a fact."

Mrs. Anna Woods, mother of Ross and Jessie Woods, walked by with a stack of folded linens and towels. She appeared to Russian Bill as a woman of dignity and class. She listened to the raised voices and confronted Ross. "There is to be no more arguing or raised voices in this hotel. Our guests expect and deserve a reprieve from the noise and trouble of the saloons and the mines."

Bean Belly started to leave, but Ross called out to him. "And stay away from my sister."

Jessie Woods looked up from her chores. Anna Woods noticed Russian Bill standing at the registration counter and wondered what this very unusual-looking man wanted in her hotel.

"Ross," she said, "there is a, um, gentleman who might need your assistance, please."

Ross watched Bean Belly leave the hotel. Then he walked over to the counter and addressed Russian Bill. "Mister, that's a very flashy outfit. It's none of my business, and pardon me for saying it, but let's just say that Shakespeare can be a rough place to get along in."

Russian Bill smiled and removed one of his guns and placed it on the desk, the grip side showing five notches facing up, right under the nose of Ross Woods. "Yes, I couldn't help notice that you were having problem with that tremendous fat man."

Pointing to the notches he continued. "Last one was for Apache that was chasing a man-lady. Famous outlaw said maybe that one not should count. But what could I do, I already carved. Maybe just I should leave it for the next white man. What do you think?"

Ross Woods considered this for a minute. Then he said, "How can I help you?"

"If it wouldn't be too much trouble," said Russian Bill, "I would like a room."

CHAPTER 33

The largest adobe building in Shakespeare was a classy saloon called the Roxy Jay. It was evident that money had not been spared in the rich decorations. Russian Bill stood inside the swinging doors and marveled at the difference between this drinking establishment and the Gem in Galeyville that seemed to be preferred by Curly Bill and his friends. The Gem had a simple covered board between two whiskey barrels. A couple of medium-size mirrors, framed like oil paintings, hung on the walls. But the Roxy Jay had a full-length, polished, mahogany bar accompanied by a full-length mirror. The room was also decorated with a wood plank floor, brass spittoons, twenty lamps, and many gilt-framed pictures hung tastefully on the wall. Add to this atmosphere a side room with billiard and card tables, and you had the makings of the most popular resort for the men of Shakespeare.

Russian Bill sat alone at a corner table and fussed with his hair. Every few minutes he signaled for more whiskey. He was feeling the effects and smiling from time to time, and was not dwelling on the rejection experienced with Curly Bill.

Two men appeared wearing tweed jackets and well-worn hats and stood before his table. Russian Bill reached for his guns, but did not pull them.

The first man removed his hat. "Mind if we join you, mister? If you say no we kin jus' move along. If you don't want no company we would understand and our feelin's wouldn't be hurt. Or mebbe yer waitin' on somebody, and . . ."

Russian Bill stood up and removed his hands from his guns. "For sake of heaven, sit down already."

The two men sat down at the table and Russian Bill joined them. The two men said their thanks, and Russian Bill waited. When neither of them spoke, he asked, "Is there something I can do for you, gentlemen?"

The two men looked at each other. The one that had spoken before shuffled in his seat. "Well, we was wonderin' if you might be interested in investing in some gold and silver mines." Russian Bill stood up, wobbled a little, and waved for the attention of the bartender. He held up three fingers, and with a sweep of his arm indicated that he was buying drinks for the two men now sitting at his table. Then he sat back down.

Russian Bill shrugged and ran his fingers through his hair. "Gentlemen, I would like for you to have drink with me. Then tell me if you think I am fool, or maybe you think I was in basement when they handed out brains."

The man that had done all the talking said, "No, mister . . ."

Russian Bill interrupted him. "Ah ah ah," he said, waving a finger. "First drink, then talk."

There was an awkward moment where the three men looked at each other while they were waiting for their whiskey. The mine sellers looked concerned, but when Russian Bill smiled at them, they relaxed and smiled back.

The bartender arrived with a tray. He set three glasses filled with whiskey on the table. Russian Bill put some coins on the tray, and the bartender went back to the beautiful mahogany bar.

Russian Bill, still smiling, raised his glass. The mining men awkwardly did the same. Russian Bill downed his whiskey in one large gulp. The other men did the same.

Russian Bill pounded his empty glass on the table. First, the talking miner pounded his glass in a similar manner, then the other one followed.

Russian Bill pulled on his mustache. "Now, gentlemen, do you know what was the first thing I see when I arrived in Shakespeare?"

"No, sir," said the talking miner.

Russian Bill grabbed his empty glass, studied it then turned it upside down on the table. "Two men," he said. "One was son of hotel lady owner, and other was enormous, fat man. They argue about sour mine deal. It is funny thing. I go to Tombstone, where there is much mining for silver. I go to Charleston, where refinery is for Tombstone silver. I go to Galeyville, where they also have mines. I go to Willcox, where they . . . no, Willcox only have cows. But I go to all these towns and nobody wants to sell me mines. Come here to Shakespeare, see argue two men over bad mine deal. Same day come here, two more men want to sell me mines. So I ask again, gentlemen, do you think I am fool?"

"Well, mister . . ."

"My name is William R. Tettenborn. Friends and outlaws call me Russian Bill."

"Tetten . . . Tetten . . . if it's all right, kin

we jus' call ya Bill?"

Russian Bill turned his glass right side up. "Yes, that might be fine if you don't try to sell me bad mine deal."

"Well, Bill, thank you fer the drink. I'm Obed, Obed Foote, an' this here is Alexander Stevensen."

Russian Bill chuckled.

"Obed Obed Foote. That is funny name. Tettenborn is funny name too, but Obed Obed Foote might be funnier. And your friend Alexander who don't talk have Russian name, no? Possibly have father or mother from Russia?"

Obed Foote took off his tweed jacket, hung it on his chair back, and loosened his collar.

Then he snapped his red suspenders. "Do you mind, Bill?"

Russian Bill said, "Please be comfortable. You too, Alexander."

Alexander kept his jacket on but loosened his collar.

Obed Foote said, "It's true that Alexander ain't one for idle talk and gossip, but if ya want to know anythin' at all about rocks, or prospecting or mines, why then he's yer man."

Alexander Stevensen removed his hat. "My people came from Denmark. They settled in Utah with a lot of other Danes. Utah had been under Mexican control just prior. I came here about ten years ago when the first silver strike was just about played out."

Suddenly four *angels of the night* entered the Roxy Jay Saloon through the swinging doors. Immediately the patrons applauded, whistled, yahooed, and made other sounds of approval and delight. The angels spread out. One went to the bar, one threw her arms around a cowboy at a table, one opened a shot-full-of-holes door that separated the bar from the billiard and poker tables. When she entered that adjacent room, the door quickly swung closed. The fourth angel spotted Russian Bill and quickly and smoothly eased herself onto his lap.

She ran her fingers through his hair. "You sure got purty hair, honey. Say, what's your name? I don't remember seeing you before." She sniffed his hair and put her face in it. "Ooh," she said. "Your hair smells so good."

Russian Bill removed his hat and gently slid out of the chair. "Please, miss, permit me the honor of purchasing for you choice of poison. Please come to bar with me. Then you must allow me to return to business meeting with these gentlemen."

She looked up and for the first time noticed that there were others at the table. "Howdy-do, Obed. Hey, Alexander."

Obed smiled. "Hello, honey bunch."

Alexander said, "Howdy, powder puff."

The angel stood up and was all over Russian Bill. As quickly as he unwound himself from her arms, she wrapped him up again. She chuckled and said, "Say, honey, where are you from anyway?"

Russian Bill escorted her to the bar. "I am from faraway place called St. Petersburg in Russia. May I please ask where you are from?"

"Well, ain't you the polite one? Sure you can ask, honey. I'm from Deming, and I'm from Lordsburg up the road here, and Silver City. You might say I'm from everywhere but here."

They made their way through the crowded, smoky room and stood at the bar. Russian Bill asked, "Why not from here, too?"

The angel looked at him. "You might ask your business associates. They'll set you straight."

Russian Bill glanced over at Obed and Alexander. They were busy talking to each other.

Then he turned back to the angel. "Well,

Miss Powder Puff Honey Bunch, I would put value on your opinion of those men I sit with as to honest miners, since you know them."

"Well imagine that," she replied. "No one ever valued my opinion on anything before, honey. But if you really want to know, I would judge them to be mainly honest and reliable, and very successful, too."

Russian Bill thanked her and told her that she was very beautiful and kind. He especially liked her light-brown hair and her green eyes, and he told her that the violet dress she wore was nice, too. He motioned for the bartender and asked him to serve her anything she wanted and to kindly bring more whiskey to the table for his guests and himself. He gently removed the angel's fingers from his hair, examined himself in the massive bar mirror and teetered back to his table.

He seated himself and said, "Lovely lady suggested I inquire with you gentlemen why she lives in many places, but does not reside here. I am curious."

Obed Foote had the answer. "It's like this, Bill. Shakespeare's a different kind o' town from what you've seen in Tombstone an' them others. It's the only place I know that has no school, no church, no bank, no newspaper, no club, and no plumbing.

"There used to be a lot of crime here, mostly from the bigwigs. When the first big silver strike petered out, some of the owners thought of a scheme, an' they salted the desert with diamonds. Some o' their own men made it public that they found all these diamonds out in the desert while prospecting the area. Purty soon ever'body was comin' here to get in on it. There was so much publicity that men like Baron Rothschild, and generals like Dodge, McClellen and Butler, came here to invest. Arizona was also invaded by thousands of prospectors and amateurs alike who dreamed of uncovering fields of diamonds.

"But Alexander here was one of the first to figger it out that it was nothin' but a big plot for the original investors to git their money back, and mebbe make a few bucks to boot."

Russian Bill smiled. "How did you know this, Alexander?"

Alexander laughed. "Once I examined a couple of the diamond samples, the answer was simple. You see, Bill, these diamonds were already cut. They do not exist like that in nature."

Obed nodded and took over the conversation. "So it was a big scandal. The swindlers fled for their lives, and the investors and prospectors went on home to wherever they came from. Then Alexander and some others found more silver. It was mostly low grade, but there was so much of it that it paid to mine it. Meanwhile there were problems with Apaches, and then came Johnny Ringo and Curly Bill, the Clanton Brothers, the McLaurys and other outlaws."

Alexander said, "So it was every man for himself until very recently when some of the concerned citizens organized a group they call the Shakespeare Guard. They have an arsenal of guns and ammunition over at the general merchandise store, and old Nick Hughes, who owns the butcher shop, has agreed to provide his meat locker as a jail until a proper one can be built."

Obed snapped his red suspenders. "The Shakespeare Guard made it clear that they won't put up with any, well, with any women like Honey Bunch over there. Oh, they kin come t' town whenever they want, but the same carriage that brings them in has to take 'em out at night. They can't stay over. Do ya understand?"

The bartender appeared with a bottle and began to fill the three glasses. Russian Bill asked him to please leave the bottle. He tossed some coins on the tray. The bartender conveyed his thanks, as Russian Bill had been providing generous gratuities all night.

Russian Bill filled the glasses to the rim. The men clinked them carefully without spilling so much as a drop. The drinks were quickly downed, culminating in a chorus of *ah*s.

"You see, Bill," Obed Foote said, "we didn't think you were no fool. It's jus' that nobody but miners or men with mining interests come to Shakespeare. That is except for a few hustlers and outlaws, but anyone kin see that yer not none of them."

Russian Bill thought about that for a few seconds. Then he poured another round. Alexander Stevensen said, "So, Bill, the question then becomes what brings you to Shakespeare?"

Russian Bill's smile slowly melted as he considered that question and all that had happened in the past few weeks. He lifted his glass. "I could not go where I wanted to go. Where was most important place for me to go. So I decided to come to town named for greatest poet in the world, William Shakespeare."

They drank their whiskey and Russian Bill poured again. "When destiny does not provide straight path, man must ignore brain and follow heart. I heard this place,

Shakespeare, mentioned one time in passing. I did not know of mining or anything else, only the name. From that alone, I think my heart led me here."

The mining men looked at each other.

Obed Foote spoke first. "So, Bill, Alexander and I want to show you somethin'. Do you 'spect to be busy tomorrow?"

Then Alexander said, "Say, Bill, do you happen to have any other clothes?"

CHAPTER 34

The next day, Russian Bill and his new associates wound their way through a narrow underground passage in a silver mine called Hamlet. They were dressed in rough miner's clothes, which Russian Bill had to purchase at the general merchandise store before riding out to the mines.

The young man who assisted him, John Phillips, marveled at his regular white, fringed buckskins. He said he had never seen anything like them and wanted to know all about them, who had made them and how had Russian Bill come to obtain them. He said he had a curiosity about things like that. Then he picked out some canvas overalls and a long-sleeved cotton shirt. He was a good salesman and suggested underwear, socks and other items until Russian Bill said no more.

Inside the mine they each carried a candle in a twisted-metal candleholder. Obed also brought a pick, and Alexander held onto a shovel and a satchel for carrying ore samples.

Deep inside the tunnel Russian Bill asked, "What's that strange smell?"

Obed and Alexander both answered at the same time, "Guano."

Russian Bill stopped walking and turned around. "What's that?" he asked, while looking at the shadows they cast on the mine-tunnel walls.

Obed said, "Well, Bill, how do you feel about bats?"

"Govno!"

Obed shook his head. "No, it's guano. And these here bats won't hurt you. There's not more than a few dozen in this mine. Alexander's been in some in New Mexico that have thousands. Take my advice and don't even think about them."

Alexander pointed up ahead. "Let's keep going," he said, "we're almost there." They walked around a corner and stopped in a wider area of the tunnel. Alexander held his candle next to the wall on their right. A six-foot-wide vein of silver was exposed, and it ran down the wall at least twenty feet. Russian Bill noticed this, but he moved his candle all around in every direction looking for bats.

Alexander handed Russian Bill a pick and took his candle. "Chip off a hunk of rock from anywhere in that vein, Bill."

Russian Bill looked around the vein. He selected a spot and swung the pick. Sparks flew and some rocks fell to the ground.

Alexander took the pick and handed Russian Bill back his candle. "Now, Bill, Obed and I are not going to touch those samples at all. You pick up anything you want tested and you hold onto it at all times. When you have them tested, you'll know that they are typical of the vein, and unaltered. We want you to trust us so we can do a lot of business together for a long time to come."

Russian Bill picked up a large rock and a small rock and placed them in Alexander's satchel.

Obed said, "Show him the other, Alexander."

"Here, Bill, you carry the satchel. And look over here."

They held their candles up to a huge vein of silver, extending from just below the ceiling to three feet above the floor. Alexander instructed Bill to take a whack at that vein.

Russian Bill again swung the pick. This time a small rockslide fell to the floor. He picked up an extra-large rock and showed it to the others.

Alexander Stevensen said, "Okay, let's get out of this tunnel and take a ride over to the assay office."

CHAPTER 35

Breakfast was being served in the dining room at the Stratford Hotel. Around the big dining-room table sat Russian Bill, Obed Foote, Alexander Stevensen, Ross Woods, Bean Belly Smith, a saloon owner named J. T. Black, and a miner named Greaves. They were eating and conversing about the price of silver ore and other mining matters.

Jessie Woods entered the room and all talking stopped. All eyes fell on her. She carried a coffee pot and a tray. The tray had a basket of warm biscuits and a plate with one fried egg, sunny side up. She set the coffee pot and the basket on the table and picked up the plate with the single egg. She held it for a moment while the guests passed the biscuits.

"Morning, Jessie, darling," said J. T. Black.

"Howdy, Jessie, darling," said the miner named Greaves.

Bean Belly Smith said, "Hey, Jessie, is that

my aig ya got there?"

Jessie smiled and locked eyes with Russian Bill, who immediately smiled back. She turned back to the table and said, "Mama told me to give this to Ross and no one else."

Bean Belly squirmed in his chair. "Come on now, Jessie. I done tol' your mama I wanted aigs this morning."

"Mama said there's only one, and I should give it to Ross."

Bean Belly pounded the table with his fist, rattling the china with a loud clanging. "That ain't right. I damn well ordered aigs. Ross never said nuthin'."

Russian Bill wiped his mouth with the linen napkin. He stood up and addressed Bean Belly. "Why not eat delicious food and leave young lady alone? She only does what her mama say."

Bean Belly stood up, the blubber on his stomach rubbing against the table and rattling it, again clattering the china. "Stay out of this, fancy man. Ain't none of it your affair."

"You want me out of it, I stay out of it. Just leave pretty darling alone."

"Or what, fancy man? You gonna shoot me with those fancy carved guns? Well, I gotta gun, too, mister. Not anything like yours, but it'll get the job done, yessiree."

He pulled an old gun out of his overalls and pointed it at Russian Bill. "I told you to stay out of it, fancy man."

Russian Bill lifted his coffee cup and with an unshaking hand took a sip. "Why you want to point gun and say names at me? You don't know me. I don't call you anything, even though it is easy to think of many names to say."

J. T. Black wiped his mouth. "Sit down, Bean Belly. Let us eat in peace. My ulcer is running in circles here."

"Y'all want to eat in peace? Jus' tell Ross there to pass over that aig, and then tell fancy man to sit hisself down and shut the hell up. Once all that happens, you kin all eat in peace."

Ross Woods held up the plate with the egg. "Let me get this straight, Bean Belly," he said. "You want me to pass this to you, and then when this man sits down we can all eat in peace?"

Bean Belly sat down. "Yes, and hurry up. It's probably cold b'now."

Ross held the plate up. He paused, then quickly slurped up the egg. Before Bean Belly could react, Ross threw the plate at him, striking him in the face. Bean Belly shouted, stood up and managed to fire one round at Ross.

Ross was hit in the chest and immediately slumped to the floor.

Mrs. Anna Woods heard the shot and ran into the room. She saw her son lying on the floor with blood soaking his shirt. "Ross, no! Oh no!"

Jessie Woods fainted. Everyone at the table except Russian Bill dove for cover. Russian Bill lunged at Bean Belly.

Bean Belly yelled, "Get off me, you foreigner sumbitch!" He fired another shot. That one struck Russian Bill in the foot. Then he stood and pointed the gun at Russian Bill, who was on the floor, contorting in pain. He put the gun away and faced Mrs. Woods. "I'm sorry, Mrs. Woods. I didn't mean to shoot him. I jus' wanted that aig is all."

Bean Belly turned his back on the dining room and walked out of the Stratford Hotel, his smoking gun at his side.

Mrs. Anna Woods rushed to Ross while Russian Bill crawled to Jessie.

CHAPTER 36

Russian Bill sat on the end of his bed upstairs in his room. He was dressed only in his white, fringed pants. Two bloody towels covered the floor under his feet. He was looking at his foot and contemplating using his Bowie knife to dig the bullet out of his instep. There was a feeble knock on the door. Russian Bill set the knife down and reached for his holster. "Who knocks?"

"It's me, Jessie."

"Jessie, come in, please."

Jessie opened the door and timidly peeked inside the room. Russian Bill motioned her in. She entered and closed the door. She tried not to look at Bill, as he was not wearing his white, buckskin shirt, but she could not help herself. When she spoke, it was in a soft voice. "My brother is dead. My mother is crying in her room. A wagon was fetched and they took Ross to the undertaker."

She wiped a tear from her eye and looked at Russian Bill's foot. "How bad are you shot?" she asked.

Russian Bill could not help smiling at her. "I just finished cleaning foot. Bullet is shallow, probably going through leather boot helps. Boots were special made and cost twenty-four dollars. I will promise you to not rest 'til I make fat man pay for killing brother and hurting you and your beloved mother."

Jessie pulled a chair up to the bed and sat down facing Russian Bill. "There's a group of men. They call themselves the Shakespeare Guard. Some of them are already meeting. Why not let them go find Bean Belly?"

"I must do this after bullet comes out. Will you help dig at it with knife? It is not deep. Look, you can see it."

"Don't you need whiskey or something to help with the pain?"

"No. I must keep head clear." He paused and looked at Jessie. "You are most beautiful young woman, but you know already because they all say 'Jessie, darling.' You know all the men adore you."

"I still would like to hear you say it. Say 'Jessie, darling.' "

Russian Bill smiled. "Jessie, darling."

Jessie hesitated, having difficulty finding the words, and being embarrassed to express her feelings. She gulped and said, "I don't really know you, but I can't help it. I get this funny feeling every time I see you."

Russian Bill looked down at his foot and blotted some seeping blood with one of the towels. "Funny feeling like I make you laugh?"

"No, Bill. I think the funny feeling is because I'm falling in love with you."

"This can't be true, Jessie. All these men, everyone here adores you. You can't possibly fall in love with me over all of them."

Jessie's brown eyes sparkled. "I only know what I feel, Bill."

Russian Bill stood up. "Jessie, darling, I have loved you since I saw you when I first came into Stratford Hotel. My heart beat so fast I could hardly breathe. And it's doing it again now."

Jessie Woods stood up and faced Russian Bill. "So is mine."

Jessie fell into Russian Bill's arms. He held her tightly and stroked her long, brown hair.

CHAPTER 37

It was early in the morning and all was quiet at the Stratford Hotel. Jessie paced around the darkened lobby, lit by dimmed lamps, lost in thought and prayer, torn between grief and excitement.

She placed crocheted doilies on the arms and backs of the cushioned chairs, looked around to be sure she was alone. She spoke tentatively, in short phrases, as she busied herself with chores that were left undone.

"Dear God. I don't know if I even have the right to pray to you. There is no church here, and I have never in my life set foot in one. Although I have listened to some preachers who were riding the circuit. I never knew my daddy but that's all right, because Mama has always given me her love. Now she has lost her only son and I lost my only brother. Mama is up in her room crying. I have never seen her cry before. She is a very strong woman, but now

I think she could use some guidance and assistance to get through this loss.

"If you could see your way clear to help her get through these times I would be grateful and beholden and I know Mama would, too. If you can't help her yourself, maybe you can provide the right words to me so I could give her at least some comfort."

Jessie emptied each of the many ashtrays into a bucket, and then scrubbed them spotless with a damp cloth.

"If Ross is there with you now, please know that he is a good boy. He always looked after Mama and me, and was respectful. Even though he also didn't go to church, and liked to drink whiskey and smoke cigars, and maybe gamble a little and spend money too freely, he was still a good son and a good brother. He was a good person who didn't deserve to have everything taken away from him at a young age.

"That circuit preacher said that you welcome everyone to your house in the sky. I know you will like Ross. Could you let him know how much Mama and I already miss him and will always love him and will never ever forget him?

"I'm sorry to take up so much of your time, but I have one more subject to cover and one more request. Thank you for bringing Bill into the Stratford and into my life. I truly believe that the timing was not an accident. He loves me and will help me get through my brother's loss. I already love him so much! Now he's going after Bean Belly, the one that killed our Ross. Please protect William from harm, and bring him safely back to me.

"I know I am asking for an awful lot, and don't have the right to. Mama is a good woman, but very stubborn, and I'm afraid she will never ask for any consideration from anyone. Thank you very much for listening to me."

Jessie wiped a tear from the corner of her eye. She walked over to the registration counter to open the big ledger. She wanted to look at Bill's signature one more time and run her finger over it. But before she was able to accomplish that, the front door opened and Otto Johnson walked in carrying a baby wrapped in blankets. When he saw Jessie at the desk, he walked over. "Jessie," he said. "Thank God you're here!"

CHAPTER 38

Russian Bill limped to the dining-room table, where Obed Foote and Alexander Stevensen had already started eating their breakfast. J. T. Black drank coffee. Mrs. Anna Woods stood by with a coffee pot.

She said, "Sit down, Mr. Tettenborn. Let me pour you some coffee. How is the foot this morning?"

Russian Bill pulled out a chair but did not sit down. "My dear Mrs. Woods, thank you for concern. This is second time I am shot. Other time in Fort Worth, Texas, I am shot in leg. That was worse injury than this one. Also stabbed in shoulder in Denver. That man who stabbed shoulder and other man with gun, well they don't eat breakfast anymore, ever. And, if I have anything to say, that Bean Belly who shot beloved son Ross will soon be eating breakfast in hell for eternity."

"Thank you, Mr. Tettenborn," Mrs. Woods

replied. "But please, you have already been hurt. Nothing you can do will bring back Ross. I don't want any more bloodshed."

Russian Bill sat down. "The bard, William Shakespeare himself, said 'Blood will have blood,' Mrs. Woods. I heard that Bean Belly already rode off and the Shakespeare Guard is after him. I will soon leave and see what I can find."

At that moment, Jessie Woods entered the room carrying a baby. Russian Bill stood up and stared, dumbfounded.

"Don't everybody look so surprised," Jessie said, looking happy and very much like a mother. "Well, she's not mine. I'm just watching her for Otto Johnson. In case any of you don't know, Otto's wife died giving birth to this beautiful baby girl, Mattie. Otto bought a milk cow so that she could have her milk every day. Well, yesterday someone stole that cow, and Otto thinks it was one of Curly Bill's men, who he noticed looking at the cow yesterday. He asked me to watch Mattie and he lit out after him about two hours ago."

Russian Bill took a big sip of coffee and set the cup down in its saucer. "That's nice of you, Jessie. Thank you, Mrs. Woods. I must go now, but I will soon return. Did Otto Johnson say which way he was going?"

"To San Simon, just over the Arizona border. Please be careful."

Mrs. Woods did not miss the significance of Jessie's plea, nor the look that the two of them had exchanged. She glared at her daughter with an expression of disapproval.

Russian Bill turned to Mrs. Woods. "Thank you again for coffee and wonderful hospitality, especially considering the tragic cold-blooded murder of your son." Then he turned to the table. "Gentlemen."

He tipped his hat to Jessie and Anna Woods and walked out of the hotel.

CHAPTER 39

Russian Bill urged his horse forward at a moderate clip on a good solid trail leading west. A desert landscape of drab and unexciting creosote and mesquite bushes, the thin-armed occatillo with its vicious thorns, an occasional palo verde tree, fishhook and prickly pear cacti, and always tumbleweed. The sand was a rich, reddish brown. A range of mountains flanked the northern distance.

He slowed to a walk and began talking to himself. "What are you doing, you crazy Russian? Why do you talk so much? They never believe you. They think you lie about everything, and still you keep talking. Curly Bill and that Ringo, they think you lie because you can't do anything right. Those new business partners, they are not interested in you. You know that they care only about money you invest to get silver out of mines. And what of this Jessie? Why do you speak feelings to her? Curly Bill, he would not speak feelings."

There was a rider up ahead, so Russian Bill cluck-clucked to move his horse along. Moving swiftly did not slow down his self conversation. "Curly Bill, John Ringo, they don't talk many words. They do actions. You need to be like them. Do you listen? But you love Jessie, don't you? Yes, I love her. So what is wrong with telling feelings under circumstances of falling in love? Maybe it is too soon for such talk. But she say to you her feelings. That is true, but she is woman."

Russian Bill cluck-clucked again and soon he approached the rider. When he attained shouting distance he yelled, "Hello on the trail. Do not worry, I am friend." He urged his horse along and galloped to the rider. The horses then both slowed to a walk.

"I am William R. Tettenborn. Are you Otto Johnson of Shakespeare?"

"Yes, I am," said Otto Johnson, with a note of concern in his voice.

"I have just come from there."

"Is everything all right with my Mattie?"

Russian Bill smiled. "Yes, she is a beautiful baby, too. Your Mattie, she is in very good, very safe hands. And Miss Woods, Jessie, who look after sweet baby, she tell me about cow, and how you go find Curly

Bill and get cow back."

Otto Johnson adjusted his gray hat. "That is correct, sir. I bought that cow so I can get milk every day. What do you think would happen to that baby with no mama and no milk?"

"No, Otto Johnson, I know you are doing right thing, but Curly Bill and gang . . . well, how do you think they will act when you demand cow back if you find it?"

Otto Johnson rubbed his chin whiskers. "Mister, right now I don't much care. I put all my spare money in that cow for my little girl, and if they won't give 'er back, well then they might as well kill me, 'cause I don't want to be around and watch my baby suffer. I'll tell you this, if they don't give her back, I'll take out as many of them as I can before they kill me. You can count on that, I swear."

He paused and took a long look at Russian Bill. "Yeah, I b'lieve I've seen you in Shakespeare. Either that or I'm getting you mixed up with pictures I've seen of Buffalo Bill. Know what I mean?"

"That's a good one, Otto Johnson, I've never heard that before."

"Mind if I ask what you're doin' out here?"

Russian Bill pointed to a large jackrabbit

that crossed the trail in front of the horses and dodged around a creosote bush before squeezing itself down a hole. "You know Jessie Woods's brother, Ross, was killed. I was shot in foot at same time. Custom-made boot was ruined. Fat man called Bean Belly done it. This morning I hear Shakespeare Guard go look for him in Lordsburg and Deming. May go on to Silver City, too. But to me that seems too stupid, even for jackass like him. I have feeling he may go this way. We will see."

They both urged their horses into a gallop and took off toward San Simon. In a short time they came upon a rickety, weathered sign reading "San Simon." A loud buzzing sound spooked both horses, which fussed and kicked. In the shady shadows of that sign was a large, coiled diamondback rattlesnake, flicking its wet, black tongue and positioned to strike.

They easily rode out of striking distance and the snake held its ground. Otto Johnson pulled his gun and looked back, but he thought better of the situation and reholstered it. Then side by side they rode on.

Soon they came up to a large ranch with a corral near the entrance. Before they had the chance to dismount, two riders were upon them. These were Joe Hill and Jake

Gauze, two of Curly Bill's men. They both had their guns drawn.

Joe Hill said, "Reach for the clouds."

Russian Bill and Otto Johnson threw their hands in the air.

Joe Hill asked Jake Gauze to get their guns, so Jake rode up and collected the hardware and leather.

Joe Hill studied both men. Then he said to Russian Bill, "You the one they call Russian Bill?"

Russian Bill smiled. "Curly Bill I think had difficult time with Tettenborn."

Otto Johnson was puzzled. "Russian Bill? You in with this lot?"

"No," Russian Bill said. "I am reject."

Joe Hill indicated Otto Johnson with a nod and asked Russian Bill, "Who is he?"

Otto Johnson urged his horse forward a step. "He doesn't have to answer for me. I am Otto Johnson. I am a hosteller for the National Mail and Transportation Company. I live in Shakespeare with my baby daughter. Her mama died giving birth. I am here because the cow which I bought so's to have milk for my baby somehow wandered all the way here to your ranch." He pointed to the left side of the corral. "I believe it is that Jersey over there in your corral."

Joe Hill removed his hat and scratched his head. Russian Bill looked at Otto Johnson, smiled and nodded his head in approval. Joe Hill waved his hat high in the air, a signal to some of his associates.

Jake Gauze said, "We will see about that cow, Mr. Johnson. Just sit tight for a couple of minutes. Russian Bill, I sure do admire that horse of yours. I don't suppose you'd consider a sale or trade?"

Russian Bill patted and stroked the white horse's neck. "I thank you for compliment of horse, but I don't think so. Do you know young man name of Jim Hughes?"

"What about Jim Hughes?"

"Meet him on trail one day when first going to Galeyville. He liked horse very much. He also offered trade."

Joe Hill and Jake Gauze looked at each other, then they began laughing and slapping their knees.

Suddenly there was a loud clap of thunder and the sky darkened noticeably. As if it were a proclamation from a higher authority, Curly Bill, John Ringo, Jim Hughes and Billy Breakenridge rode up.

Curly Bill smiled. "Well, looky here. It's Russian Bill. Hey, Jake, give these men back their guns. There ain't gonna be any trouble here."

Jake Gauze rode over and handed Russian Bill and Otto Johnson their belts and guns.

Russian Bill said, "Thank you, Curly Bill. So nice to see you again. Looks like your jaw is healing good. How do you feel?"

"Never better."

More thunder sounded as a summer storm was moving over the Chiricahua Mountains.

Russian Bill said hello individually to Ringo, Hughes, and Breakenridge. In response Jim Hughes smiled, Billy Breakenridge bowed his head slightly and touched his hat. John Ringo was amused and puffed on a cigar.

Curly Bill asked, "Who's your friend?"

"This is Otto Johnson. He's from Shakespeare."

Otto Johnson removed his hat and wiped his hair back with his hand. "I prefer to speak for myself, Curly Bill, if it's all the same to you."

"Sure, Otto Johnson, what's on your mind?"

"I need milk to keep my baby daughter alive 'cause her mama died. My cow wandered off and made its way here. That's her in your pen over there. The Jersey with the heart-shaped spot on her left hindquarter."

Curly Bill lit a cigar. "Joe, bring that cow

179

out here! Jake, who brung it here?" Jake Gauze leaned forward and swatted a fly away from his horse's head. "I do believe it was Tall Bell."

Curly Bill puffed on the cigar. "Go find him and bring him here."

More thunder erupted and it began to rain.

For the first time Billy Breakenridge spoke. "How's the outlaw business, William?"

Russian Bill frowned. "All I can do is express disappointment. How does tax collecting go?"

"The deputy tax collector is escorting me back to Tombstone with just under three thousand dollars in taxes for the new county. Best decision I ever made was to enlist Curly Bill, and I never would have gone through with it if I didn't run into you in Galeyville, when you said something about wanting to speak to him."

Russian Bill wiped rain off his face. "Glad to hear it worked out for one of us. If it's not personal, where did you go collect taxes?"

"Well, as you can imagine, I'm not at liberty to divulge specific locations."

Curly Bill said, "That's right."

"But I will say that we rode into a lot of

canyons and hide-outs where there was cattle of dubious ownership. Curly Bill introduced me to some of his associates in variations of this speech: 'Boys, this is the tax collector from the new county and I am his deputy. Since we are all law-abiding citizens here, we know that the government cannot be run without we pay our fair taxes.'

"Curly Bill knew about how many head of cattle they each had, and if they hesitated or said they had no money, he made them give me a banker's order. He told them if they ever got arrested it would be a good thing to show that they were taxpayers in the county. Curly had many a good laugh over their reactions."

By then it was raining heavily. Jake Gauze returned with Tall Bell. Joe Hill brought the cow over to Otto with a rope lead.

Curly Bill puffed out smoke and addressed Tall Bell. "Did you appropriate this here cow from Shakespeare?"

Tall Bell wiped his wet face and looked around. "Come on, boss, you know I did."

"Well, did you know that this cow is the only source of milk for this man's orphan infant?"

Tall Bell said that he didn't know that. He said that to him it was just a cow.

In the rain Curly Bill said, "We steal from

Mexicans. We steal from men with large holdings. From stages now and then, and even from the government. But I'll be damned if we steal milk from babies."

Here he paused like a judge to consider the case. He puffed more smoke and addressed Tall Bell again. "You will take this cow back to the Johnson home. And on foot. In the rain. Without your guns. Hand 'em over. I don't care if it takes you three days to get there. We'll look after your horse. Jimmy Hughes might want to go visit his ma. All right, Jim?"

Jim Hughes nodded. Tall Bell unstrapped his gun belt and handed it to Jake Gauze.

Curly Bill instructed, "Now, Jim, you ride along and keep an eye on Tall Bell. If he harms, or tries to harm, Otto Johnson in any way, you have my permission to shoot him." Tall Bell whirled around and faced his leader. "Oh, come on now, Curly Bill, that ain't fair."

Curly Bill said, "Hit the trail."

"Much obliged, Curly Bill," said Otto Johnson. "Next time you're in Shakespeare, I'd be proud to show you my little Mattie, if you'd call."

Curly Bill used his scarf to wipe rainwater off his face. He looked at Otto Johnson. "You can count on it."

The procession began heading east in the rain: Tall Bell on foot leading the cow by the rope, Jim Hughes, then Otto Johnson. Russian Bill remained at the ranch. When the others were well on their way, he rode up close to Curly Bill.

He said, "Corral is not so full as when I was here last time, after opportunity trip to border."

Curly Bill smiled, and Russian Bill continued. "When you go to Shakespeare, do you know a fat man they call Bean Belly?"

"Yeah, I know that big ol' side o' beef. What about him?"

"In Stratford Hotel he kill Ross Woods because mother only have one egg. She give it to Ross but Bean Belly he wanted it. They argue. Bean Belly then shoots Ross. I jump on Bean Belly, pound his fat face and try to take gun, but he is strong for fat man and shoots me in foot. Mrs. Woods, the mama, and Jessie, the sister, they cry and grieve. I am on quest to kill fat Bean Belly sumbitch. Shakespeare Guard, I hear they go look for him in Lordsburg, Deming, maybe Silver City. I don't know why but I have feeling he run this way. You don't see him around here, do you?"

Curly Bill blew out a stream of smoke and watched raindrops break it up. "That barrel of shit passed through here yesterday. He said he was headed to Willcox. You might try Foxey's Saloon. Remember where we played poker? If he's not there, he'd be easy enough to find. Just ask if anyone's seen a walking tub o' lard."

Russian Bill removed his hat, turned it over and watched the rain spill off the crown. "I remember Foxey's Saloon from poker game in third chance to prove worthiness. Thank you again for giving me so many chances. I think I will find this Bean Belly."

He hesitated but then added, "There's one more thing. I don't have anyone to tell, so I will tell you. I think I am in love."

Immediately he regretted sharing this personal information with Curly Bill. *Why must you talk so much,* he thought.

"Russian Bill in love. Well fancy that," Curly Bill said. "Who's the lucky girl?"

"Jessie Woods, sister of the boy that died."

"Jessie Woods? Well, Russian Bill, I hate to disappoint you, but everyone's in love with Jessie Woods. She's the darling of the miners and the cowboys alike. And you'll have a tough nut to crack with her mama. She wants Jessie to marry young John Phillips, one of the clerks in the general store. Seems mama doesn't like outlaws for Jessie."

Russian Bill said, "What is this?"

Curly Bill laughed. "She chased several of the boys out of the hotel with a broom. No, that Anna Woods is one proper lady, and she wants her daughter to maintain that high level of propriety."

CHAPTER 40

The rain came down steady as Russian Bill made his way to Willcox. What Curly Bill had said about Jessie and her mother worried him, and he talked to himself about it as he rode westward through the rain.

"Mrs. Woods, she doesn't like outlaws for her daughter. So you are not an outlaw. Everyone says that is so. Outlaws say you are too much gentleman for outlaw life. Doesn't that go good for proper lady, Mrs. Woods? These miners and cowboys, they use sleeve to wipe mouth. They have no manners, no upbringing. They shoot and kill over single egg. And what of Jessie? She is darling of all miners and cowboys, but does she adore them back? And what of this young clerk? How can he afford to support a wife and maybe a family? I have done well, so far, as mine speculator. And what of love between Jessie and this John Phillips? If Jessie loves him, how is it that she confesses love to you? These are important questions for understanding situation with darling Jessie."

The rain stopped momentarily and Russian Bill wondered how long it would take to arrive in Willcox. It was approaching sunset, and the cloudy western sky was magnificent in vibrant reds, blues, black and white. The big, white horse had no trouble galloping or walking on the soggy trail.

He expected that they were only a few miles from Willcox. A meal and a drink would sure be satisfying after a day's ride. Maybe a big steak and some whiskey. "Leave the bottle, please, my good man." That would have to wait until he found his man and the business was concluded.

"Now you get near Willcox, why don't you think of Bean Belly, you crazy Russian? You only let Jessie in your thoughts. You better be careful or you will get yourself killed. You need to make smart plans in your dealings with Jessie and Bean Belly. Otherwise it will be easy for you to get hurt. Yes, I will make plan for Jessie before I marry her. And I will make plan for Bean Belly before I kill him."

CHAPTER 41

It was well after dark by the time Russian Bill hitched his horse in front of Foxey's Saloon. The summer monsoon had blown over, and the hard rain had faded to a steady drizzle. An occasional lightning flash illuminated the mountains in the distant north. Although he was soaked, he was not cold. Now he was on track again, thinking only of his purpose.

Foxey's Saloon had two entrances. Russian Bill stood before the swinging doors of the main entrance on the corner of Railroad Avenue and Maley Street. The other entrance was through a traditional side-door on Maley. He stared at the doors, checked his guns, took two steps forward, and then stopped. He imagined what would happen if he found his man inside.

In his imagination he walked through the doors and spotted Bean Belly sitting at a table, drinking and talking to a young lady.

The bartender stood behind the bar pouring something from a water pitcher into whiskey bottles through a funnel.

"Hello, Bean Belly, you murdering sumbitch," Russian Bill shouted.

The young lady stood up and ran out through the side door.

"You killed Ross Woods, only twenty years old, and you shot me in foot and ruined good boot. What do you say for yourself?"

Bean Belly said, "I'm sorry, Russian Bill. Did you come here to murder me?"

"What do you think?"

Bean Belly said, "I see how it is. Well, do you mind if I take a swallow first?"

Russian Bill nodded. "Go on."

Bean Belly looked around. Then he broke the whiskey bottle on the table and charged at Russian Bill with a tremendous roar. Russian Bill easily dodged the charge like a matador in his prime, and Bean Belly slumped down on the floor crying. Russian Bill cocked his gun and fired.

But that was only a thought. Russian Bill found that he still stood in front of the Foxey Saloon's doors. He shook off the images of Bean Belly lying on the bloody floor and took two steps forward. Once again he stopped to consider how it might happen inside.

This time when he walked through the swinging doors he found Bean Belly standing at the bar. The young lady stood next to him. The bartender smoked a black cigar. Bean Belly turned to watch Russian Bill.

He said, "Well look who's here. Hello, fancy man. I've been waiting for you." Then Bean Belly brought up a terrible, ghostly laugh and said, "All right, let the Russian sumbitch have it!"

He began firing at Russian Bill. So did the young lady. For good measure, the bartender pulled a sawed-off shotgun from behind the bar and let loose with both barrels. Russian Bill was hit multiple times before managing to squeeze off a shot. He collapsed on the floor in a pool of blood and gore.

Back on Railroad Avenue, Russian Bill said, "*Govno,* shit. Why you must think so much?"

He checked his guns again and walked into the saloon. Bean Belly was drinking at the bar. The bartender stood with a rag and watched Russian Bill.

Russian Bill said, "Hello, Bean Belly."

Bean Belly turned and said, "You!"

"Yes, it's me. I have come for satisfaction for murder of Ross Woods and shooting of my foot. Never mind what you do to expensive leather boot. You, bartender, don't dare reach for gun behind bar."

The bartender lifted his arms. "No, sir, I got no hounds in this hunt."

Russian Bill nodded, then turned to Bean Belly. "You, Bean Belly, go out in street. I prefer to not provide blood and broken glass to this man's place of business."

"Thank you, sir," said the bartender, using his rag to rub like crazy on the bar top.

In a smooth and swift move, Bean Belly yanked a Bowie knife from his boot and threw it at Russian Bill. Without waiting to see if his target was hit, Bean Belly ran out the side door onto Maley Street. The knife had sailed by Russian Bill's ear and stuck in the wall behind him. Russian Bill gave chase.

By the time he got out the side door, Bean Belly was already halfway down the block. Russian Bill shouted, "Stop running, you fat, murdering coward sumbitch!"

He took careful aim with his pistol and fired at Bean Belly. The shot missed badly, but broke the glass on a street lamp just where Bean Belly was running. A falling shard cut deep into Bean Belly's left cheek, just below the eye. He stopped running and grabbed at his bloody face.

"You shot me!" yelled Bean Belly, puffing

and wheezing.

"Drop your gun and I might allow you to live."

Bean Belly thought about it, and then threw his old gun in the street. He covered his bloody face with one hand.

Russian Bill picked up the gun. "Do you swear to never set foot in Shakespeare again?"

The question gave Bean Belly cause to be hopeful. "Yes, I swear."

Russian Bill stood next to Bean Belly. "Shakespeare Guard, they look for you and may not stop for long time. They want to put you in butcher shop meat locker temporary jail. Then they will put you on trial, but not regular court trial. This will be Shakespeare Guard trial where their minds are already made up about what you did. If I was you, I would want to stay away from area where Guard might look. If I let you go, it is with understanding that I will personally kill you if I hear talk of you returning anywhere near Shakespeare, or if remaining Woods family is harmed in any way. Do you understand and agree?"

Bean Belly was even more hopeful. "Yes, I understand and agree."

Russian Bill glared down at him.

"All right, I will let you go. Dr. Morse, his

house is just around this corner. He can take care of your face and your foot."

Bean Belly removed a filthy scarf and applied it to his free-bleeding cheek. "My foot? Ain't nothin' wrong with my foot," he said.

Russian Bill placed his gun against Bean Belly's right boot. He fired. The sound of the gunshot coupled with Bean Belly's prolonged scream broke the stillness of the night.

CHAPTER 42

After the business with Bean Belly was concluded, Russian Bill went to the hotel, and had that steak and whiskey he had craved back on the trail. Although tired and a little stiff from the earlier ride, he was satisfied with the way it had gone with Bean Belly and content with the food and drink he had just consumed.

He considered spending the night in the hotel, but the boarding house where he and Curly Bill had stayed had a pleasant, widow-lady owner, and his room had been comfortable. So he rode over there. Before long he was looking in the mirror in the same room that he had when he nursed Curly Bill.

He removed his boots and considered the pain in his foot from the bullet wound. It throbbed, and the gauze that Jessie had wrapped it with was blood-soaked. Russian Bill was also unhappy about the condition of his hair, which hung limp and slightly greasy from the long ride, the dusty trail and the rain. The foot and the hair would both need attention in the morning. First would come sleep in a comfortable bed.

The feather pillow was soft, and so were the thoughts Russian Bill had of Jessie Woods. Oh, that she could be there now, sharing that warm and comfortable bed, as Mrs. William R. Tettenborn. What was that quote from William Shakespeare about love at first sight? *"Hear my soul speak. Of the very instant that I saw you, Did my heart fly at your service."*

He remembered how she had come to his room to speak of her brother, but then the conversation had turned. She had asked him to say *Jessie darling.* It was a matter of routine that everyone called her that, but she specifically wanted to hear him utter it. *Say "Jessie darling."* He had said it, and the next thing he knew they were both empty-ing their hearts to each other. Then she fell into his arms and he had hugged her for the longest time. He had dared to plant a kiss on top of her head, as she was a full head shorter. He had caressed her long, straight, brown hair, ran his fingers through it, bent his knees slightly and pressed his face to hers, smelled her fragrance, and finally pulled away enough to stare at her large, brown eyes.

As Jessie was leaving his room, she had turned and had quickly given him a peck on the cheek. Then she had run out of the room, excited and embarrassed at the same time. Russian Bill thought of these instances and others as he pulled the heavily feathered pillow in close and almost immediately drifted off to sleep.

CHAPTER 43

On the outskirts of Willcox, Russian Bill saw smoke coming from a ranch house. It was too much for a fireplace, and a fireplace would not normally be used during the summer in southeastern Arizona, so Russian Bill was concerned that something was wrong. He urged his horse on, and as he neared the house he saw that it was on fire. Three Apaches were riding back and forth outside.

Russian Bill reached for his rifle, leveled it on his arm and took a shot. One Apache went down. *"Govno,"* he said, surprised. The other Apaches began firing arrows in his direction. One stuck in his saddle right between his legs. Two others whizzed by so close that one of the feathered ends brushed against Russian Bill's ears as it shot by.

As he neared the cabin, Russian Bill tried dismounting before the big, white horse was fully stopped. That caused him to fall, and he hit the ground hard, sending the rifle flying near the cabin steps and rattling the entire left side of his body. From the ground he pulled both guns and started firing. He could see that there were several dead Apaches in various positions near the cabin, including the one he had shot. Unsure if any of his bones were broken, he continued firing his pistols, one at a time, at the Apaches, while telling himself in Russian that his body may not be able to take any more tumbles after this one and from falling from a moving train.

He aimed carefully and fired again, and another Apache fell to the ground. Russian Bill crawled to his rifle near the cabin steps. Using the steps as cover, he took careful aim and squeezed the trigger. Just like that, the last Apache fell.

Russian Bill rose to his feet and was relieved to find himself fully intact. No bullet holes, no arrows sticking out, no broken bones. His foot throbbed, but that was from a different fight. The roof and one of the side-walls of the cabin were on fire. He ran to the front, where the door opened and a familiar figure ran out coughing and holding tightly onto a rifle and a bundle.

"What took you so long, William?" she

managed to say and then had a coughing attack.

When she regained most of her composure she said, "Don't go in there. They're all dead."

Russian Bill went inside anyway. Thick smoke prevented him from seeing, and the blasting heat from the spreading flames seared his lungs. He tried sweeping smoke away by flailing his hands and caught just a glimpse of a pair of small feet under a table. He lunged forward and grabbed at them. With a strong pull, the young body slid out. He couldn't see much, but he instantly knew that the child was a young girl, about seven or eight years old.

He made his way outside and took a long breath of fresh air. Then he looked at the dead child in his arms and noticed the arrow in her side. He gently set her down in the dirt away from the burning cabin.

"William, your shirt — it's on fire!"

Russian Bill saw flames moving up his left sleeve and started to feel the burn. He quickly pulled the shirt over his head, threw it on the ground, and stomped on it.

For the first time, he looked and found that the voice was coming from Lana Harris, the lone rider from his first trip to Charleston. She was removing the blanket wrapped around an infant and was quietly sobbing.

He turned to her and removed his hat. "It is my old friend Svetlana. You sob because baby is dead?"

"No, William, I sob because the baby is alive." Russian Bill was overcome with emotion and turned away to wipe a tear from his eye. He looked at his arm, which had turned red from the burn. Then he looked back to Lana. "Why you always bring Apaches with you?"

She smiled and gently placed the infant over her shoulder and patted its back. "Maybe it's better to ask why you always parade around with no clothes on everywhere you go."

Russian Bill picked up his shirt, shaking his head. "*Govno,* shirt is dirty and burned. Some fringe was shot off in Charleston by Sandy King, who ride up and down the street shooting. Now more fringe is burned." He paused to look at a very dirty and disheveled woman in men's clothing holding a baby over her shoulder. "It's good to see you, Lana Harris."

He brushed off his shirt with his hand and pulled it on. He walked up to Lana Harris and, taking care to not disturb the baby, gave her a hug.

CHAPTER 44

Lana explained that she was on her way to the ranch of Colonel Henry Clay Hooker to deliver some correspondence about a cattle deal. She had seen the Apaches approaching the cabin and had raced to get there in time to help. The little girl had opened the door for her and had been immediately struck by an arrow. The child's parents were already dead. Only the baby was sleeping in a cradle.

There was only one dead Apache when Lana had situated herself and began shooting. She had killed three more. Lana didn't know if an arrow had knocked over a lamp or if the Apaches had set the fire. She was having trouble breathing and she ran out of ammunition. That's when she wrapped the baby in a blanket and pulled the little girl under a table. She heard gunshots and looked out to see a man in white buckskins fall off his horse and begin shooting everything he had at the Apaches.

"This is the second time you've saved my life against the savages, William. I don't trust there will be another."

They had found a broken shovel in a small vegetable garden near the cabin, and Russian Bill had managed to dig a deep enough hole to bury the unfortunate child. The arrow had been removed, and Lana had wrapped the girl in Russian Bill's saddle blanket, which he insisted on providing.

When she was covered, Russian Bill and Lana Harris each said a few words. Russian Bill said, "God above, please take this little girl special in your arms. She was brave here on this little farm, and now she is in your care. If it is your will, please reunite her with her mama and papa so they can be together in your house. We will take baby to doctor and try to find loving home. Oh, yes, and thank you for protecting me from broken bones when I fall from train and off horse, and for guiding Apache arrows away from me and Lana, and for setting shirt on fire and not burning beautiful hair. Shirts can be replaced. Well, most shirts can, anyway. Thank you."

Lana Harris gave Russian Bill a sideways look, and added, "Heavenly Father, thank you for sparing this little one's life; thank you for sending William here to help us out. Like William said, the little girl was brave here on earth. So were her parents. We would be grateful if you will accept them all and show them eternal peace. We ask you humbly and remain your servants. Amen."

Russian Bill asked Lana if she could ride the few miles back to Willcox while holding the baby. She said she sure could. "You'd be surprised to know what I can do on a horse."

Russian Bill pulled the sleeve up on his shirt and looked at his arm. It was red and throbbing. He took the baby while Lana climbed up in the saddle. She reached down and took the infant in one arm. Then Russian Bill mounted up.

They rode toward Willcox side by side. Lana said, "William, I'm glad you took my advice about getting off a quick shot. And your shooting is accurate, too. And you also listened to me about sentence structure. You are much easier to understand now. At least your language is. I'll never understand what a crazy Russian is doing out here riding around Arizona saving women and children from harm."

CHAPTER 45

"Emergency, emergency!" Russian Bill yelled at the front door of Dr. Morse in Willcox. Lana Harris was by his side holding the baby, which had slept for most of the ride but was now beginning to stir.

Dr. Morse opened the door and looked at the dirty and disheveled couple on his porch. "Come in, come in," he said. "I should have known it was you. It's always you. I only had one case recently that didn't have anything to do with you. That was last night. Big, fat fella came in, shot himself clear through his foot in an accident. Said he didn't know the gun was loaded. Wish I had a nickel for every time I heard that one. What seems to be the problem today?"

Lana looked at Russian Bill. "All right if I explain, William?"

Russian Bill nodded.

"We just had a real bad fight with a party of Apaches. The family out there all died except this baby. The Indians are all dead, too. William and I buried a little girl, about seven years old. The cabin burned, along with the mama and daddy. This baby should be checked because she hasn't fussed much and dang if we know what to do with her. Also, when you finish with her, I know William won't say anything, but would you please check his burned arm. It looks all red and blistering. He ran into that burning cabin and pulled out that little girl so she could be properly buried. As you can see, his shirt caught fire, and his arm is burned."

"And how about you, miss? What is your name and what is your condition?" Dr. Morse asked.

"Oh, I'm fine, thank you, doctor. My name is Lana Harris and I just have some smoke in my lungs, but I'm feeling pretty well under the circumstances."

Dr. Morse gave Lana a stern look. "All right, young lady. I'll get around to examining you in good time." He then turned to Russian Bill. "You, Mr. Tettenborn, you wait here. You, Miss Harris, bring the infant in here, please."

Lana Harris gave Russian Bill a nod and a wave, and followed the doctor into the examining room. Russian Bill sat in a stuffed chair in the parlor. His arm was stinging and his foot throbbed. The left side of his body was sore and he had a headache. When he closed his eyes, a picture of the little girl they had buried popped out like the images had on the Holmes stereoscope he had seen in St. Louis.

Next thing he knew he was awakened by Lana waving a paper fan at him. "Wake up, William, your turn to go in there."

Russian Bill sat up with a start. "What happened? What did doctor say?"

Lana Harris put her hand over her mouth and coughed. "He says we should notify the sheriff immediately. He said the baby is remarkably well. She needs milk, but being a cattle town there are dairy cows here. He had a little and gave it to her, and she drank it all. He knows that that family were recent settlers from the Indian Territory out Oklahoma way. He doesn't know if they have any kin, but listen, William, he knows a young couple that want a child. He's going to ride out there directly, and I'm going with him. William, this couple has a nice ranch and they raise horses and a few head of cattle. Doc Morse thinks they will be very happy to have this little baby. But in case they're not, there are several widow women here in Willcox that will care for her until a proper home can be found or some kin come looking for that family.

"The doctor said I'm showing a few signs of inhaling smoke, which I know I did. My throat is hoarse, my eyes are red, and I'm coughing up mucus. He's giving me an elixir for that. He needs to check you for that and take a look at your arm. Then, William, I am going to ride with him out to that couple's ranch in his buckboard. We're going to stop for some supplies first. So as soon as you get checked out, you can notify the sheriff and then you can go on your way with my thanks and the thanks of that precious little baby. Of course, you are welcome to ride out to that ranch with us if you'd like."

Lana Harris bent down, grabbed a handful of Russian Bill's hair to pull it out of the way, and planted a kiss on his cheek. "Now get in there," she said, "and do what you're told. There is no time to waste."

CHAPTER 46

Russian Bill accompanied Lana Harris and Dr. Morse into the Norton-Morgan Commercial Co. on Railroad Avenue. His burn had been treated with a cooling antiseptic cream and his arm was wrapped tightly with bandages. His bullet wound had been cleaned, and his foot had been wrapped. Dr. Morse said it was healing satisfactorily under the circumstances of Russian Bill refusing to lie down for a few days. The doctor noted that Russian Bill's entire left side was badly bruised. Fortunately there were no broken bones or dislocations, but the pain and stiffness was likely to get worse before getting better. He was given a dose of laudanum and a full bottle to take along for pain. They were now all inside the store and Russian Bill was feeling a little light-headed.

Lana held the baby, wrapped in a blanket. Dr. Morse had some milk on hand and had warmed it. The infant girl readily accepted it in the quarter-moon shaped bottle with a rubber nipple. The doctor also had some cloth on hand that Lana had been able to fashion into a diaper. Now they were shopping for supplies. Lana approached Mr. Norton while Russian Bill made sure he walked clear away from the displays of oranges and soap. He also kept an eye, blurry as it was from the laudanum, out for the all-black cat that had caused him so much grief on his last visit.

While Lana and Dr. Morse were speaking to Mr. Norton, Russian Bill busied himself browsing around the store looking for any items that might be helpful for the baby. Before long he found a basket that could be used as a cradle, a couple of small blankets, a small, brown, soft bear and a baby rattle. He brought these items to the counter and found that the doctor and Lana had put aside soft cotton fabric that could easily be made into diapers, some bottles and nipples, a supply of milk, and a couple of outfits the baby might wear until others could be made. Russian Bill quickly offered to pay.

Mr. Norton looked up. "Say, I remember you. How is it with that vein of gold? It was the Isabella mine, wasn't it?"

Russian Bill was surprised. "You have

good memory, sir. Please note that this time I don't destroy store, but actually spend money. How is black cat?"

"Yes, sir, that was quite a commotion you caused that day. Since your visit the cat has been a mite leery of customers, so she's sleeping up high somewhere around here."

CHAPTER 47

Russian Bill did not accompany Lana and Doc Morse. He was woozy and unusually tired. He went back to the boardinghouse, secured his old room for one additional night and went right to sleep. In the morning he had a large breakfast of ham and eggs. Then he rode over to Doc Morse's residence.

"Come in, William," Doc Morse said when he heard the tap on his door. "This is the first time you didn't holler 'emergency, emergency' on my porch."

"How is the baby? Were people happy to see it, or they didn't want it?"

"William, I've never seen anything like it. The wife was so happy. She was thanking God and Jesus and Miss Harris and me, and the tears were streaming down her face. She held onto that child and couldn't stop staring at her. Miss Harris told them that it was you who saved the child and they decided to name her Billie after you."

Russian Bill smiled. "Just what is needed in west, another Bill. Do they have cow for milk?"

"No, they don't, William, but they will have one today. This couple has livestock to sell or trade, and they have a good relationship with a nearby dairy farm. Don't worry about that baby. She has a family that really wants her."

"And what of Lana? Where is she now?"

"She told me last night that she would be on her way to the Hooker ranch first thing this morning. I imagine she is well on her way. She didn't know if I would see you but she sure spoke highly of you."

Russian Bill turned to leave. "Thanks for everything you did, Doc Morse. Is gold double eagle enough payment?" He placed the large gold coin on a table in the entryway. "I go back to Shakespeare mining town where I have sweetheart waiting. I will try not to bring more patients."

As he walked out the door, Doc Morse said, "Be safe, young man. Keep well in mind and body."

Russian Bill mounted his horse and removed his hat. He ran his fingers through his yellow hair. "As William Shakespeare said, *Farewell. God knows when we shall meet again.*"

CHAPTER 48

Jessie Woods had completed her morning chores. She had told her mama that she was going to check on baby Mattie Johnson, but had instead met Russian Bill in front of the Grant House stagecoach station. They openly strolled along Avon Street side by side. They passed some shops and saloons, and stopped at the livery stable where Russian Bill's horse was being cared for.

Russian Bill resisted the temptation to kiss Jessie. He didn't want there to be any talk that might reflect badly on Jessie or Mrs. Woods. He asked Jessie to wait outside. Then he brought the big, white horse out on the street, where he put on a show only for her. First he removed his hat and combed his hair. Then he ran the hand-carved comb through the horse's mane. Using verbal commands and arm gestures, he coaxed the horse to paw at the ground, bow, and neigh. For the finale, Russian Bill dropped his hat on the ground and bent down to pick it up directly in front of the horse. In the bent-over position the horse neighed and nosed him in the rear hard enough to send him sprawling into the street. Jessie laughed and hugged the big horse's neck.

During the demonstration Jessie had seen the bandages and asked what had happened to Russian Bill's arm. As they continued their walk he recounted his adventures, starting with the most recent fight with the Apaches and ending with his encounter with Bean Belly Smith.

Jessie stopped walking. "Did you shoot him?"

Russian Bill smiled. "First I cut him, then I shoot him. You won't have to worry about seeing him anymore."

They continued walking past the barber shop. The barber, in a white apron stood outside his shop smoking a cigar. "Good morning, Miss Jessie," he said.

Jessie smiled at the barber, and Russian Bill tipped his hat as they walked by.

"Haircut, young man," the barber called out. "There's no waiting right now and it sure looks like you can use one."

"No, thank you, my good man," said Russian Bill. "Not this day. Maybe some other time."

After they had walked the full length of both sides of Avon Street, they stopped in front of the stagecoach station and gazed into each other's eyes. Russian Bill's eyes were as blue as the richest azurite that Jessie had ever seen mixed in with silver ore from the local mines. Jessie's were large and rich, dark brown like the finest of chocolates that Bill had sampled in Belgium when his party had toured that country. And the brown was a precise match for her beautiful long and straight hair.

Russian Bill said that the baby Lana Harris had rescued made him think about having a family. And he asked what her thoughts were on starting one.

"I love children, Bill. I'd love to have some. Taking care of Mattie I think brought out those kind of thoughts in me, too. But, Bill, there's something I need to tell you that has me worried."

"Jessie, what is it?"

"It's Mama. She doesn't miss much of what goes on around her. She knows about us, and she doesn't like it. I'm afraid she might try to interfere."

Russian Bill remembered what Curly Bill had told him. "Look here, Jessie, don't worry. I will soon have talk with her, and then I know she will approve."

Jessie looked up and down the street. "I better get back, Bill. I don't want to, but Mama hasn't been the same lately, and she needs my help. Thank you for what you did. I mean with Bean Belly. And what you did to help that poor baby."

Jessie looked around again. The barber had gone back inside his shop, and the street was nearly deserted. She gave Russian Bill a quick peck on the cheek, then hurried to the Stratford Hotel without looking back.

CHAPTER 49

Russian Bill stood before a mineshaft with Obed Foote and Alexander Stevensen. They held miners' tools. A sign read *No Trespassing, James Crittenden Owner.*

He removed his white hat that, ever since it had been pierced by the vaquero's bullet, had grown progressively dirtier. He pulled his hair out of his face and addressed his companions. "You gentlemen have many mines, some with me and some in other partnerships. And you own a few of your own. With your permission I would like to buy this one on my own with some of the profits from first mine deal. The one with the few dozen bats flying around making guano mess on floor. If Alexander approves of this investment I would like to register this as Jessie Darling Mine."

Obed Foote chuckled. "I'm glad yer learning it's much easier buyin' and sellin' mines than workin' 'em."

Alexander nodded. "If I were you, I'd buy this one. I've seen enough to know. Then I'd purchase the adjacent claim. Crittenden owns that one, too, and he hasn't begun to dig. I expect you could turn these over quickly as a pair. The ore is likely low grade, but there's lots of it, and you already know that we've shown on many occasions that low-grade ore can be extremely profitable when there's a bunch."

"Say, Bill," Obed said. "Jessie Darlin' suits this silver mine real good. You must still be sweet on Jessie Woods."

"Gentlemen, I will confide that I have never before felt this way. I try to think of other things, but I only think of her. I think I am crazy in love."

Obed and Alexander laughed, and Russian Bill joined them.

Alexander set down the pick and shovel he was holding and snapped his suspenders. "That's wonderful, Bill. When do you intend to pop the question?"

"Each few weeks I have been writing to Mama in Russia. Postmaster in general merchandise store, he help me send. I ask she send me simple gold Russian ring. I only give hint about beautiful woman with long, brown hair like goddess, and large, brown eyes like puppy dog. When ring come

I will have talk with Jessie and Mrs. Woods. Meanwhile I try to get rich in silver-mine business."

Obed fanned himself with his filthy hat. "Well, Bill, when the dust settles on these transactions, Alexander and me, we want you to join us down at the new strike they call Stonewall. It's a day's ride southeast, right near Mexico. We're going there to scope it out."

Alexander smiled. "All indications are it's a real dilly."

CHAPTER 50

Twelve men sat on wooden chairs in the smoky basement of the general merchandise store in Shakespeare. The Shakespeare Guard was meeting. Jackson Price stood before the membership.

"By now you all have heard that the capture of Bean Belly Smith has eluded our posses. There are rumors circulating that he was dispatched over the state line in Arizona by one of Curly Bill's men, possibly by the one in our very midst who is known variously as Russian Bill and William Tettenborn. But this man has bragged so much and told so many wild stories of the people he's met, killed or is related to that it's impossible to take anything he says as fact. Especially since nobody, but nobody, has ever seen him do anything except get shot in the foot."

Jackson Price paused to light a cigar and take a few puffs. "Having said all that, I believe it's best for us to keep an eye on him and continue to be watchful for any other suspicious persons in or around our town. Now, Robert Hart will give his report on the small party of Apaches that was spotted on the road between Lordsburg and Deming."

CHAPTER 51

Mrs. Anna Woods and Jessie Woods sat on stuffed chairs in the elegant lobby of the Stratford Hotel. Russian Bill stood before them. Occasionally he paced. He looked at the mother, then the daughter. Then he looked at the mother again. At last, he gathered the courage to speak.

"Mrs. Woods, Jessie, thank you for meeting here with me. Mrs. Woods, your name I believe is Anna, no?"

Mrs. Woods tugged on her sleeve. "Yes, it is, Mr. Tettenborn. Why do you ask?"

Russian Bill stopped pacing and began unconsciously running his fingers through his hair. "Please forgive observation that in Russia, where you know I come from . . ." He began pacing again. Jessie watched him, amused at his nervousness but concerned about her mother.

Russian Bill twirled his hair with his fingers as he continued. "In Russia we have beautiful name of Anya, translation Anna, meaning of favor and grace."

He stopped pacing and faced Mrs. Woods. "Mrs. Woods, I have need to ask question of you, and hope you will consider what I am about to say, and show true value of favor and grace with positive reply."

"Now Mr. Tettenborn . . ."

Russian Bill interrupted her. "Please, Mrs. Woods, hear me. I want to tell you truth of my life before I ask important question for graceful answer."

Mrs. Woods squirmed in her chair.

"In Russia my mama is cousin to Czarina and is member of royal court. I am lieutenant in Royal Hussars, which is Russian army. I have trouble with superior officer over gambling money he owed me. He laughed at me in front of other officers. When I later find him alone, I try to talk to him again but he laughed and spit. I could not longer stand it and I strike him and knock him down. He went crazy and said he would have me discharged. This would be disgrace to my mother. We fight more and I kill him. I did not mean to kill him, but fight go too far and he died.

"This happened several years ago. Around that time a diplomatic trip was organized for Grand Duke Alexei Alexandrovich.

Mama used influence for me to go on trip as part of support group. We go through many countries, and I see Paris and Brussels and London, and several others in Europe. Then we go to New York and Washington where there were many elegant parties for Grand Duke and entire delegation."

Jessie smiled as she imagined the parties. Mrs. Woods sat with no expression. Russian Bill continued. "Arch Duke, he have fantastic time. In Washington we go on tour. We meet President Ulysses S. Grant and General George Armstrong Custer, and also General Philip Sheridan. To enlighten Arch Duke about American frontier, we travel long distance through many states where a buffalo hunt was arranged for all, and the guide was Buffalo Bill Cody himself. We talk for long time and become friends.

"Also Sioux Indian chiefs were there. Grand Duke, he kill big buffalo. Indians make beautiful buffalo hide blanket for him from killed buffalo to always remember hunt. They make clothes for me. Very special, very soft, from hides of many deer.

"After hunt we go to St. Louis. Here we see many wagons gathering supplies to go to American west. After while, Arch Duke and group move on with tour of Mississippi

River and New Orleans, but I remain in St. Louis. I stay there and read novels and newspapers of west. Mama also send me books and magazines from Russia.

"Best of all she send me new Russian novel called *Anna Karenina.* I bring that up because there's your name again, Mrs. Woods. That brilliant masterpiece of literature was written by friend of mine who is Russian count named Leo Tolstoy. But mostly I read about American west, and hear about outlaws like Curly Bill and many others."

Anna Woods stood up. "This is very interesting, Mr. Tettenborn, but I'm afraid I have work, and I . . ."

Jessie Woods yelled, "Mama, please!"

Russian Bill said, "I know I stall asking question because of great importance. I will ask now, Mrs. Anna Woods . . ."

He took a deep breath. "I, William R. Tettenborn, declare that I am delirious in love with your darling daughter, Jessie."

He realized that he was fussing with his hair, and he dropped his hands to his sides. "Mrs. Woods, I have done some things I am not proud of. But now I am trying to change and live productive life. I am doing well as mine speculator. I have savings and plan more to get with big deal in works. I promise to always love, respect and care for Jessie with all my heart, if you, and this is finally previously mentioned question, if you will give us blessing for marriage together."

Russian Bill fumbled in his pocket and fished out a dazzling gold band embellished with precious and semiprecious stones.

Mrs. Woods spoke right up. "Mr. Tettenborn, I am sure that Jessie is flattered by your attentions and your proposal, but I'm not able to give you my blessing. You are an outlaw and a killer of men. You say you are trying to live a productive life, but experience has taught me that a leopard does not change its spots."

Jessie began sobbing loudly.

"And what of the men you killed or harmed, and your outlaw friends? You may be wanted by the law and not even know it. Or your life could be at risk, and so could my Jessie's, by the family and friends of your victims. I've lost my only son, Mr. Tettenborn, and, regardless of your good intentions, I do not intend to lose my only remaining child to violence, or have her become a young widow. For these reasons I cannot and will not give you my blessing. I ask that you respect my decision and do not prolong your stay here at the Stratford. Please discontinue your courtship of Jessie immediately."

Mrs. Anna Woods walked out of the lobby. Jessie Woods lowered her head and cried.

Russian Bill stood stunned for a long moment. Then he walked out of the hotel without looking at Jessie.

CHAPTER 52

John Ringo and Jim Hughes rode into town from the southwest. Jim Hughes stopped at his father's butcher shop about halfway through town. Ringo rode to the general merchandise store at the far end.

Jim Hughes's mother, Josefa Hughes, ran out of the shop to greet him. She hugged her son eagerly.

Ringo hitched his horse and tipped his hat to two ladies who were exiting the store. Then he walked in. He found a young clerk and informed him that he needed to buy a new pair of boots. The clerk directed him to an area around two large displays. There he found a pair of black leather boots. He held them out at arm's length, glanced down at Ringo's feet, looked at the boots he was holding, and set them down. He looked around and found another pair. These he showed to his customer.

"What do you think of these?"

Ringo glared at the young clerk. "I hate 'em."

The young clerk quickly put them down. "I'm sorry, sir. Is there something in particular you're looking for?"

"Something easy on the eyes as well as the feet. Something a little more special."

The young clerk smiled. "I understand, sir. I believe I have just the pair." He picked through a pile of boxes and came up with a pair of black, high-shank riding boots with some fancy tan stitching.

Ringo took them over to a wooden chair of the same style that the Shakespeare Guard used in the basement. He sat down, removed his old, worn boots and tried on the new pair. He stood and took a few steps. "Kinda tight."

The young clerk said, "They are made of calfskin, and calfskin will stretch. Kinda form to the shape of the feet."

Ringo glared at him again as he took a few more steps. "You can keep the bull in the corral. I'll take these and wear them now. You can throw the old shit stompers away."

CHAPTER 53

John Ringo and Jim Hughes entered the Roxy Jay Saloon, found Russian Bill drinking at the bar, and decided to join him and see what was on his mind these days. After the greetings, Russian Bill looked around the room and saw that no one except the bartender, Ringo and Hughes was in hearing range.

"Did you boys ever love someone?" he said with a significant sigh.

"Over in Texas there was a girl when I was young," Ringo said.

Russian Bill asked what happened.

Ringo lit a cigar. "She was about as jealous as a hound bitch with her first batch of pups. Made me realize I don't like having my haunches spurred by no drip-nose of a gal. I came west with a cattle drive and escaped with my freedom."

Jim Hughes chuckled good-naturedly. "Hosses an' wimmen will shore make a man go whistlin', provided he's still young enough to pucker."

Russian Bill took a long pull from the whiskey bottle he was tightly gripping. "I am confused, gentlemen. Curly Bill, he thinks I am not enough outlaw to join gang, but here I am in Roxy Jay's drinking with two of his most important men. On other hand, Mrs. Anna Woods, she thinks I am too much outlaw to marry Jessie. John Ringo, you are outlaw with much experience. Jim Hughes, you are young but have many outlaw friends. I ask you both, what should I do?"

"If you want a thoughtful response," Ringo said, "pass over that bobwire extract."

Russian Bill passed the bottle with a noticeably shaky hand. Ringo accepted it and shook his head. "You're a trifle shaky there, hoss. How long has your foot been planted on that brass rail there, 'cause it appears that you're about to take root?"

Russian Bill looked down at his feet. "I don't know. Maybe long time."

The bartender nodded in agreement.

Jim Hughes chuckled again and said, "You keep that up an' you'll soon be seeing things that ain't there."

"I already do that," Russian Bill said. "I succeed very good at seeing what's not there. The bard who this sumbitch town is named for said *we know what we are, but we know not what we may be.*"

He pulled one of his guns and aimed it at his reflection in the long bar mirror. Immediately he was tackled by Ringo and Hughes. He kicked a little but was easily restrained.

"Hello," he said, looking up at those who tackled him and laughing.

Ringo easily took the gun out of Russian Bill's hand, and Jim Hughes pulled the other one from the holster. They handed the weapons to the bartender.

Ringo loosened his hold a little. "If we let you up, are you gonna fight?"

Russian Bill smiled, and then gulped. "Maybe if I hit you in face, you will put me out of misery."

Ringo said, "Don't think that I won't."

Russian Bill laughed. "Why do you knock me down? Do you think I will shoot myself?"

"Hey, if you want to blast a hole in your head large enough to drive a meat wagon through, well, it makes no difference to me. Jim and I jumped you because you weren't aiming at your head. You were aiming at the mirror, and that glass behind you is kind of sacred around here."

Jim Hughes nodded. "Anyone'll tell you that the bar and that huge piece of glass came all the way from St. Louis."

Russian Bill perked up. "St. Louis? I was in St. Louis."

The bartender said, "That so? The last stage of the journey, over twenty miles, was made by an eighteen-mule wagon. You won't find another glass like this anywhere in the territories."

Ringo drank from the bottle and passed it to Hughes. "When the boys get rattled and riled, they usually shoot at that door over there." He pointed to the well-perforated door separating the bar from the gambling and billiard room. Russian Bill looked at the door. Then he looked back at the long, beautiful mirror.

Ringo said, "So I wouldn't be standing around on either side of that door."

Russian Bill didn't hear him. His hat was on the bar. He was studying his image in the mirror and running his fingers through his hair.

CHAPTER 54

Over in the general merchandise store, Russian Bill looked for the postmaster, Mr. Long. He walked around through displays of foods, hardware, clothing, and other provisions and supplies, but he didn't see Mr. Long anywhere. He did see two clerks talking to each other and laughing. The same clerk who had helped John Ringo with his boots turned his way.

Russian Bill approached and said, "I need to see postmaster, Mr. Long, please."

The clerk said, "Yes, sir, I'll see if he's in the back or downstairs."

As the clerk stepped to the back, the second clerk busied himself with stock work.

Almost immediately Mr. Long emerged from the rear. The clerk said something to him and pointed to Russian Bill. As the postmaster walked up front to a desk, the clerk took a position where he could arrange a pyramid from cans of tomatoes near the front. "Hello, Mr. Tettenborn," Mr. Long said. "Please, sir, sit down over here. Are we dispatching another letter to Russia?"

Russian Bill sat down. "Thank you, Mr. Long. A small package, too. How much do I owe you?"

CHAPTER 55

The sun rose large and red in the east as Russian Bill set out for the new mining district called Stonewall. Shortly, as he rode down a southeast trail, he heard a hawk scream up high, and he saw a number of ground squirrels scurrying for cover. He looked back up at the hawk soaring with its wings fully extended, riding air currents overhead. *Why do you scream up there like that? Why not take by surprise? Dive on them. They won't see you until it's too late.*

He had covered a distance at a leisurely pace. Now he allowed the horse to walk for a while and he paid attention to his thoughts and feelings. First he wondered what Jessie was doing at that moment. Was she thinking of him as much as he was thinking of her? Would she go on with her life and give in to her mother's wishes, or would she declare independence? *But no, get real, you crazy sumbitch. How can she leave mama at time*

237

*like this? Of course she will not. You will do
well to move on with life and forget her. She
will do the same. It will be difficult but like any
loss it will be more better in time.*

His thoughts were interrupted by a very
loud buzzing. When he turned his head, a
gigantic, wasp-like creature was hovering
menacingly alongside his ear. It was as long
as one of his fingers and shiny black with
bright red wings. Russian Bill gasped.
"Govno!" But the creature tired of buzzing
around this human on a horse and flew up
the trail. Russian Bill brushed at his face
and shivered. Later, on the trail he saw one
of these wasps fighting a large, hairy spider.
It appeared that the wasp was winning the
fight, having stung the spider multiple
times. He said out loud, "Bugs fight and kill
each other."

He stopped in the shade of a rocky slope
and drank water from his canteen. Then he
cluck-clucked and moved on. When he
rounded the end of the slope, at the same
instant, an Apache appeared rounding from
the other side. Both stopped, having been
equally startled. Russian Bill pulled his gun
but did not take aim. After a brief staring
duel, the Apache moved forward. A second
horse carrying a squaw with papoose
emerged. Russian Bill held still with his gun

pointing upward and allowed the family to pass. Then he continued down the trail.

He stopped on a rise and looked down at a bustling mining operation with ore wagons, blasting, miners at work, horses and mules.

The trail sloped down and soon Russian Bill reached the living and working area of the Stonewall district. He rode through a section of shanties and tents, stopping when he saw a sign reading *Stevensen and Foote, Buy, Sell, Trade Claims, Surveying, Recording.* He began to dismount but stopped cold when he noticed another sign. This one was planted in the path between tents. It read *James Crittenden for President, William Tettenborn for Recorder.*

What is this? he said to himself.

He walked toward the Stevensen and Foote tent, and just as he was about to enter, a plump and busty woman strutted out, adjusting her clothing as she moved along. When she saw Russian Bill, she stopped. She smiled at him, looked him over up and down, and licked her lips. Russian Bill took a step back and watched her sashay down the row. Then he pulled back the flaps on the tent and looked in on a smiling Obed Foote.

Obed smiled and straightened his shirt.

"Bill, hello. Good to see you. Come in out of the heat."

"That woman, is she . . . ?"

"Yes, Bill, she is all that an' more. We're booming here, Bill. Doin' very, very well. She's one of the rewards I give myself for all the hard work."

Russian Bill smiled. "Hard work, you? Sure you do. You are sly old devil. That's what you are."

Obed smiled back. "Age is just a number. You'd be surprised what this old man can still do."

Russian Bill turned away. "Please, I don't want to know."

Obed said, "Say, I can fix you up."

Russian Bill removed his hat and fanned himself with it. "No, thanks. I came here to get away from women, and for business. What is meaning of sign for vote outside?"

"Oh, yes. Alexander and me organized the district. Well, to be honest, Alexander, he understands minin' laws so he done most of it. One of the biggest stake holders is Jim Crittenden. He was sheriff up in Silver City for a few years. We figured you already know each other from being partners in the Jessie Darling Mine in Shakespeare, and, well, we figured with the two of you teamed up for president and recorder, well, we thought we

240

could pretty much have things our way, an' we could all get rich."

Russian Bill put his hat back on. "But I know nothing of recorder duties. What must I do?"

"Right now all you gotta do is go out an' shake hands with lots of people. Tell 'em who you are and where you come from. Only leave out the part about meeting President Grant. Lots of these boys is confederates, an' they hate his guts. You should assure the mine owners that you'll be honest and speedy with filing their claims. And you're gonna have to go regular up to Silver City to record the claims and pay the filing fees. When you come back, before turnin' over the recorded deeds, you will collect your commissions. Naturally you'll meet people up in Silver City that'll ask questions and will want to buy claims. Alexander and me will have you prepared for instant transactions that you, as recorder, can record on the spot. My boy, we're all gonna make a wagonload of money."

"May I ask who I am running against?"

Obed Foote stood up and further straightened his clothing. "That's the best part, Bill. You are unopposed. Everyone is too busy wheelin' and dealin' and getting silver ore out of the ground to want the job. Now let me tell you about some fantastic claims Alexander and me got picked special for you."

CHAPTER 56

The first thing Russian Bill noticed on his second trip to Silver City was that the cattle he saw grazing around the low hills on the outskirts of town last month were still there. He did not see any cowboys watching them. They were on their own, grazing quietly in the short grass. He wondered if Curly Bill, Ringo and the boys knew about this and how they would go about adopting these neglected orphans anonymously and driving them to the Arizona ranch. Would the gang be worried that someone in town, being so close by, would see the activity? They would not want to shoot it out with these fellows, who were not Mexicans on the border, but miners, ranchers and businessmen. Who knows, there may even be some Texans living there and southern confederates. Russian Bill concluded that these cattle were likely safe from Curly Bill and his gang, at least for the short term.

The other unusual quality of Silver City was its extremely high sidewalks. There were puddles along both sides of Main Street, left over from the last storm, and Russian Bill visualized raging rivers of water surging along the thoroughfare during the summer rains. If sidewalk boards were only a few inches above the street, as in Shakespeare, Galeyville, Willcox and Tombstone, flood water would undoubtedly surge into all the buildings, raising havoc and causing much damage.

Russian Bill dismounted at the recorder's office. He high-stepped up to the boards and walked around and stretched to get the kinks out from the long ride. He found the livery across the street, and he walked the horse in that direction, intending to leave instructions for watering, feeding, brushing and resting the big, white horse. The people on the street gawked at Russian Bill and the horse. Before entering the livery, he turned to a woman in a calico bonnet with two children at her side. They were walking down the sidewalk in his direction. The children were about five- and seven-year-old boys, and both were pointing at him. He tipped his hat and signaled the big, white horse to bow to them. The woman in the bonnet smiled and the young boys jumped for joy. Then Russian Bill continued into the livery.

At the recorder's office, a county clerk saw Russian Bill walk in with a leather satchel. "Howdy, Bill. Here I thought I was gonna have an easy afternoon. Pull up a chair. Let's see what you got."

Russian Bill moved a nearby chair to the desk. He pulled out a pile of papers from the satchel and plopped them on the desk. "This is most I ever brought. There are many partnerships."

The county clerk, a balding, bespectacled man, short in stature, wearing a long-sleeved white shirt with pinstripes, the sleeves rolled up and held by garters, removed his glasses and cleaned them with a cloth he pulled from a desk drawer. "Partnerships are the most time-consuming to record. Are these all from the Stonewall district? None from Shakespeare?"

Russian Bill fidgeted with the papers. "No, I have not been in Shakespeare for maybe three months. For me there is black cloud over that sumbitch town. Anyway, I am too busy for going there."

"Okay," said the clerk. "Might as well get started."

"Let's start with my own first," said Russian Bill. "I have the St. Louis and the Silver

City mines by myself. Then there is Russian Silver mine by me and James Crittenden, your old sheriff, fifty-fifty. I have water rights to spring with sheriff again and two mill sites with Obed Foote and Alexander Stevensen. After these are twenty-six for others."

"Twenty-six? Lordy, lordy, that's a lot of activity. I was hoping to step out for a drink?"

Russian Bill produced a half-filled, clear glass flask and handed it to the county clerk along with a gold coin.

CHAPTER 57

Russian Bill entered the Antlers Saloon and sat down at a table with a view of the front entrance. The bar itself was knotty pine that was polished to a gloss. There were no fancy carvings on the bar, no backbar at all, and only three small, framed mirrors. The walls were covered with all kinds and sizes of antlers. Russian Bill had a couple of drinks and busied himself studying the antlers and trying to envision the animals they once belonged to.

He heard a commotion outside, and soon two men entered the saloon shouting. The first one was tall, thin and dirty. He wore rumpled clothing and a crusty hat. He bellied up to the bar and ordered whiskey. The second one was even taller and much heavier. He was by no means clean, but his clothes were orderly. His beige hat was nicely shaped. Right away the second man, whose name was Riley, started in on the first one, Hop Mitchell. "Did you just pay for that drink with my money?"

Quickly, Hop Mitchell downed the drink. "I don't know. You got me confused. I no longer know which money was yours and what was mine."

Riley ordered a whiskey. "Okay, let's go over this again. You said you were going over to Fort Bayard. I told you a feller there owed me money and I asked could you collect it for me whilst you were there. When you got back at first you said that you couldn't find the feller, but then you finally admitted you did collect my money, but spent it all on likker and whores. Are we in agreement so far?"

Hop Mitchell removed his hat and scratched his head. "Well, I agree with you in principle, but the problem is this. You want me to pay you right this minute, and I can't because I ain't got no money except what to live on for a few days."

Riley shoved Hop Mitchell hard into the bar. Then he doubled him up with a hard right fist to the stomach, sending Mitchell on a slow slide to the floor. "You moron," Riley yelled. "That's my money yore livin' on, not yours!"

"No, Riley, you are dead wrong. See, when I collected that money I put it separate from where my money was. And I was careful to only spend yours over at Fort Bayard."

Riley kicked Hop Mitchell. "Somebody done stole your rudder there, boy. So you was careful to only spend my money, and you was careful to separate yourn? Well, empty out yer pockets right now right there on the floor."

Russian Bill stood up. Riley turned around to face him, as he thought there might be an attempt to interfere. "Do you want a piece of this pie, Buffalo Bill?"

Russian Bill smiled and brushed his hands along the tops of both guns. "No, I don't even like pie."

Riley stared at him for a moment, uncertain about that response. Then he turned back to Hop Mitchell on the floor. There were a few coins and a couple of crinkled bills on the floor.

Hop Mitchell started to get up, but Riley kicked him again, hard in the leg. "Empty them pockets again, you miserable, lyin' sumbitch!"

Russian Bill sat back down. "Except peach. And apple sometimes, but only if it's not too sweet."

Riley turned to him again. "What did you say?"

"Well," said Russian Bill. "When you

asked me before, I forgot that I very much like peach pie. See, that is something we never get where I come from. And I also forgot apple pie if it's . . ."

"Look you, Buffalo Bill, can't you see I'm busy? 'Course if you think I'm wrong, or if you're related to this piece of shit on the floor, or if you think that getting yore britches tromped is somehow related to peach pie, just say the word, and I'll welcome you to the ball."

Russian Bill shrugged his shoulders. Riley glared at him for a long moment. Then he turned back to Hop Mitchell, who once again sat up and leaned against the bar. Hop rubbed his leg. "That's all I got, what's on the floor right now. No more kicking will produce anything else. I know I owe you the money, and I know I was a fool fer spendin' it like that. But see, this girl down there, ya know, Flora was her name, an' she put her face real close you know to mine, and the perfume or whatever got to me and b'fore I know it, I was helpless. She vamped me, or whatever you want to call it, and b'fore I know what hit me I was on the street lookin' at the moon through an empty bottle. I'll pay you the money, I swear I will."

Riley pulled his gun and flashed it at Russian Bill. Then he stuck the barrel up against

Hop Mitchell's head. "You got two weeks. I figger if you ain't got it and give it to me by then, you likely never will. And if I hear anybody laughin' about how you put one over on me, why then I'll hunt you down and decorate yer body. You got that? My fourteen dollars in two weeks or I'll squirt 'nough lead in you to make it a payin' job to melt you down."

Hop Mitchell began collecting the money that was scattered on the floor.

Riley said, "You can finish picking that up and hand it over. That's interest. You still owe the whole fourteen dollars. Understand?"

A rough-looking man wearing a suit entered the saloon. A silver star on his vest was partially exposed. "What's the trouble here?" he said to Hop Mitchell. He scanned the room with piercing blue eyes.

Hop Mitchell stood up. "No trouble, Sheriff Tucker. I was just ordering a drink and I dropped my money. Say, can I buy you one?"

The lawman was well known in Silver City as Dan Tucker, deputy sheriff. Some called him *Dangerous Dan* for prior incidents where he shot and killed before asking any questions. The deputy sheriff turned to Russian Bill. "I don't know who you are in that

251

ridiculous getup, but several citizens alerted me to some kind of disturbance between these two, I'm guessing. Will you please tell me what happened so I can put an end to it and move on?"

"Yes, officer." Russian Bill gave Riley a stern look. "I've been sitting here long time, much before these two gentlemen came in. I have seen no disturbance. They are friendly toward each other and everyone here, offering to buy drinks and causing no trouble. Only laughing and happy."

Dan Tucker said, "Are you sure about that?" Then he turned to Riley. "What do you have to say about it?"

Riley smiled and gestured with his head. "The stranger is correct. There was no disturbance. Now how about that drink, Dan?"

"Later," said the deputy as he turned to look long and hard at Russian Bill before walking out.

Riley approached Russian Bill. "I'd like to thank you, mister. That there deputy was Dan Tucker. He can be rough on us sometimes. Now belly up to the bar and let me fix you up with a whiskey and a cigar."

"That would be kindly appreciated, sir."

Hop Mitchell stood up and handed Riley the money. "Can I have a drink, too, please,

Riley? As a way of letting bygones be bygones?"

Russian Bill spent the night at the Silver City Hotel. After a hearty breakfast there, he clinked along the boards to the tailor shop. Upon entering he was greeted by a pleasant old man who looked at him at different angles. Russian Bill thought there was some medical reason for him to keep moving his head around, until he found that the man was sizing up his buckskins.

"That's quite a suit you have on, young man. Do you mind if I ask you where you got it?"

"Of course I do not mind if you ask where I got it. I got it as gift from Lakota Sioux Indians after we go on big buffalo hunt together. There were many dignitaries there. From my country Arch Duke Alexei Alexandrovich was on tour. I was part of contingency. We meet many American officers and even . . . Wait, are you from Texas or other state where President Ulysses S. Grant's guts are hated?"

The tailor smiled. "Why no, I'm from Missouri. And the war is over."

Russian Bill laughed. "I was in St. Louis long time before come to west. What I wanted to say was that President Grant, who this county I believed is named for, we all met. I shake his hand. We talk. I also talk with important generals and lieutenants like Sherman and Custer. Then we go on buffalo hunt and I become friends with Buffalo Bill Cody. Lakota see that and make gift of this outfit. But now I have many adventures and outfit is dirty, have few holes and fringe is shot off. I have come here in hopes you can help fix or otherwise tell me how."

The tailor remained smiling. "The work on that is stunningly beautiful. I would like to think that I am good, but I'm not that good. But it really doesn't matter because I don't have the hides. If you could bring me hides in the color you want, I could try to duplicate the work. I'm also afraid to try to clean it, as anything liquid may stain it and make it worse. Maybe you can travel up north some time or write to your friend Buffalo Bill. See if he can help."

"Thank you, sir. That's good idea. Buffalo Bill Cody, he travels very much a lot, but if I'm patient I think I will hear back from him."

"How about a regular suit of clothes in the latest fashion? Do you ever wear regular suits?"

Russian Bill said, "Only wear overalls in stiff material for going in mines. Very itchy.

Can't keep it on long. This outfit though is soft and pretty tough. I have worn it getting shot off horse, pushed off moving train, and shot at few other times. Thank you for your help, sir. Good morning."

When the big, white horse saw Russian Bill enter the stable, it pawed the ground repeatedly. Russian Bill noticed this and spoke to the horse. "I know you want to go. So do I. We will go for long ride together back to Stonewall mining district in few minutes. First need to find owner so bill can be paid."

CHAPTER 58

As Russian Bill rode slowly in an open area, he heard banging and clanging noises along with shouting voices and other noises that were normally foreign to the trail. At the top of a rise he looked down at the bustle of a construction camp for the Atchison, Topeka and Santa Fe Railroad tracks. The workers were a melting pot of nationalities, but there were many more Chinese workers here than Russian Bill had ever seen before.

He was reminded of many anti-Chinese signs and banners he had seen in Tombstone and other towns. And he thought of the time that Jim Wallace had called him a white Chinaman. That had bothered Russian Bill. It was one of those silly things that could either float by as so much chimney smoke or could plant itself as a dirty speck on the brain and stay there for a very long time.

Russian Bill rode down to the construction site and stopped at a tent with a crude, hand-lettered sign reading *Pork and Beans, 25 Cents.* He stopped and dismounted at the welcoming smell of a black iron pot that was simmering over a fire. Three sisters, Amanda, Nora and Madge Ownby, from Shakespeare made their living selling meals to the railroad workers and anyone else who happened by.

Amanda smiled. "Looky here, girls, it's Bill Tettenborn from Shakespeare. Where you been, Bill?"

Russian Bill took off his hat and held it to his heart for a moment. Then he placed it back over his yellow hair. "Good afternoon to you, Ownby sisters. I am elected recorder of mines at Stonewall district. I go to Silver City for business, then go back to mining activities. Can I please have some beans?"

"Sure thing, honey," said Nora stepping forward. "Hey, Madge, fix this hungry Russian a plate. That'll be two bits there, Bill."

Madge Ownby exited the tent with a plate. She ladled a generous helping of beans from the pot and handed the plate to Russian Bill along with a fork and a biscuit. "Here you are, honey."

Russian Bill dug right in. "This is good. I bet these railroad workers appreciate it. Are you here every day?"

Madge smoothed her apron. "Yes, we're

making a living doing this. So are the whore tents and the liquor wagons and the Chinese opium sellers."

Russian Bill asked how long the sisters expected to do this.

Amanda said, "Fast as they're laying tracks down, they will soon be in Deming, where they'll connect with the Southern Pacific. Then I hear they'll go all the way to the ocean in California."

"What will you do after that?"

Nora smiled and stepped forward. "We want to open a restaurant in Shakespeare." Russian Bill swallowed a mouthful of beans and finished off the biscuit. "Maybe after I finish the big mining deal I am working on, I will return and be your best customer. I haven't made up my mind yet for sure." He paused and scraped the last of the beans onto his fork. "What news is there of Shakespeare?"

"What kind of news?" asked Amanda.

"I don't know, mining. Any kind of news."

Nora took Russian Bill's plate and fork and placed them in a tub of water. "Charlie Carson who owns the sawmill up in the Burros had a fight with some Apaches, but nobody got killed."

Amanda added, "Curly Bill was in town visiting the Widow Morrison. She told me he asked about you."

Russian Bill frowned. "Yes, Curly Bill, we are old pards."

Madge said, "The Shakespeare Guard is raising money to build a proper jail and get it out of Nick Hughes's meat locker."

Russian Bill said, "I heard Nick Hughes who owns butcher shop and meat locker within is father of young Jim Hughes who rides with same Curly Bill."

Nora scrubbed the plate and fork in the tub of water. Then she dried them with a towel. "That boy will be the death of his father and his poor mother. He is always in trouble."

Russian Bill pulled at his moustache. "Oh, I don't think he's all that bad. Anyway, thanks for the beans. They were very good. Well, I guess I better ride, unless there's any more news from Shakespeare."

Madge concentrated real hard. Then she remembered. "Couple weeks ago Randall the blacksmith burned his arm real bad when a red-hot horseshoe slipped out of the pliers."

Russian Bill waited until there was a long enough pause to indicate no more news. Then he mounted his horse. "Well, thank you, dear sisters, for food and news. I hope to see you again soon."

He turned his horse around and observed the workers lay down a new section of track. Just as he was about to ride away, Amanda remembered something. She said, "Oh, almost forgot. Jessie Woods is getting married next Saturday night."

Russian Bill turned his horse around to face Amanda. "How nice," he said. "Who is lucky man?"

Amanda smiled. "It's that nice man that clerks at the mercantile store, John Phillips. Everybody says he's got a real head for business."

Russian Bill said, "Please, please tell . . ." But he thought better of saying anything else to the Ownby sisters. Instead he cluck-clucked, and off he went muttering to himself, "He has good head for business."

CHAPTER 59

It was a short ride to the liquor wagons on the south side of the tracks. There were two of them, one on each side of a whore tent. Russian Bill was not particular and dismounted at the first one he came to, but there was no business and the owner, a portly old man with a long, white beard, was sitting on a chair and snoring loudly, his head tilted to the side and his hat on the ground. On an impulse Russian Bill opened the flap on the whore tent and looked inside. Three painted ladies sat on chairs fanning themselves and chatting with each other. Small, curtained stations were located in the rear. One of the girls, a plump woman with curly, red hair said, "Come on in, honey. We won't bite."

Russian Bill tipped his hat. "Maybe later. Need drink first. We'll see." He stepped back and let the tent flap fall. It was only a few steps to the next liquor wagon. The proprietor of this establishment was wide awake. He was dressed like a bartender of a higher-class saloon, only his shirt and vest were not buttoned all the way due to the outdoor heat. When he noticed Russian Bill walk up, he smiled and said, "Well, now, I know you're not with the railroad, so you must be riding through."

Russian Bill was no longer in the mood for chitchat. "Whiskey," he said, placing some coins on the plank of pine that was set up across the wagon.

The bartender poured a full glass. Russian Bill quickly drank it and motioned for another. The bartender was willing to repeat the process, and did so again and again.

Russian Bill finally balanced a silver dollar on top of the glass, tipped his hat and walked over to the whore tent. He stood outside and remembered what Hop Mitchell said about the girl named Flora who had put her perfumed face next to his and rendered him helpless. *That would never happen to me. I am strong in mind and body. Watch, see I prove it.* He walked to his horse, which he was surprised to see he had neglected to tie up. He put his left boot in the stirrup, but just as he was about to swing on, he stopped and removed his foot.

Foot hurts real bad. Not healed yet. Heart

hurts, too. Who can say, maybe it is okay to be weak sometimes.

He led his horse to the tent and tied him to one of the tent's support poles. Then he lifted the flap open and stepped inside.

Chapter 60

Back in the Stonewall district, Russian Bill dismounted in front of his own tent. He staggered to grab his saddlebag and threw it into the tent. He removed his saddle and gear and threw all of it into the tent. He led his horse to a post where a water trough had been positioned. The big, white horse drank greedily while Russian Bill waited, shifting his weight from leg to leg. Then he moved the horse to a post near the area where stored hay was covered with a tarp. When he lifted the tarp to pitch some hay, three big tarantulas scurried out.

"*Govno!* That's all I need right now," he said out loud.

After the hay was pitched and the pile re-covered, Russian Bill charged into his tent. He quickly checked around for tarantulas. Having found none, he collapsed on his bedroll. He briefly relived his experiences earlier south of the new section of tracks.

Although it was a blur, it seemed that he had visited the liquor wagon, then the whore tent, then the same liquor wagon, then the Chinese opium sellers who also worked out of a tent. He had visited the whores again, and then made one more stop at the liquor wagon. His entire body was one big ache. *This behavior must never be repeated. This behavior must never be repeated.* Next thing he knew he was in Shakespeare.

But was he in Shakespeare? He was watching himself get off his horse and hitch him up in front of the general merchandise store. He saw himself walk inside the store and approach the clerk. This was not the same clerk who had helped him fetch the postmaster, but another one. This clerk was a little taller, a little better looking, a little . . . ? What was it that was different about him?

"Are you John Phillips?" Russian Bill asked him.

"Why, yes I am, sir," John Phillips said. "How may I be of service?"

Russian Bill glared at him and growled, "You may be of service by dying on floor in puddle of blood, you good-head-for-business sumbitch." He pulled both guns and emptied them into the clerk, blood flying everywhere, splattering his white buck-skins.

He awakened some time later in a sweat. He stood up in a panic and looked at his buckskins. They were far from clean, but there was no blood. He had a massive headache and held his head in both hands.

Had to be dream, he thought. In real life I never growl. "*Govno,* shit."

CHAPTER 61

Russian Bill was speaking to mining attorney and magnate Hamilton C. McComas in a staging area for the McComas Mining Company. He thanked Mr. McComas for allowing him to purchase a quarter interest in the Bulldog mine and asked how it looked so far.

"Better than expected. In fact, much better, Bill. The ore is assaying higher than average and there is an immense body." He rubbed his hands together and slapped Russian Bill on the back. "My boy, this looks like the one we've been waiting for."

Russian Bill smiled. "Thank you, Mr. McComas, sir. That is good news to hear right now. And how about my half interest in Sunset mine? How does that one do so far?"

McComas smiled. "You know how these things go, Bill. I'm afraid that one didn't pan out. We'll be closing that one up as soon as I can drag some men away from the

Bulldog operation. Might be awhile before that happens because we want to keep the momentum of Bulldog going strong."

Russian Bill removed his hat and ran his fingers through his long, yellow hair. "Yes, sir, I do understand," he said. "Perhaps Bulldog will make up for Sunset losses."

"Undoubtedly it will!" McComas said with enthusiasm.

CHAPTER 62

As Russian Bill made his rounds in the Stonewall district, he had to convince himself to not give in to the anger he felt. He knew that his future depended on the successful completion of several deals, and that he could not afford to botch them by allowing his motives to become suspicious in any of his dealings.

He remembered that Billy Breakenridge had told him that his boss, Tombstone Sheriff Johnny Behan, described him as a suspicious character. He had responded to Breakenridge, "Yes, it is true, I am very dangerous man. Killed many in Russia and here. I am very suspicious."

There would be no time for that kind of talk now. He was the recorder of mines, had executed the duties of his position promptly and fairly. That's how he had earned the respect of nearly everyone in the camp. Not by being suspicious.

You think too much, Russian Bill. You must clear your fool head. Do your job and complete all your deals. Then you can make your plans.

Russian Bill carefully delivered all the new recordings, taking care to smile and tell at least one story from his latest trip to Silver City. Most times he told the story of the fight in the Antlers Bar, only embellishing the ending. In his version he had gotten word from the county clerk that Dangerous Dan Tucker, the deputy sheriff, was on his way over, and everyone knew his reputation for having no tolerance for disturbances of the peace. Russian Bill had stepped in to break up the fight in the nick of time before Deputy Tucker came in.

When he got to the Stevensen and Foote tent, Russian Bill shuffled around nervously outside. The last time he had been there a plump fallen angel was just leaving, having visited Obed Foote. In his mind's eye he pictured her looking at him and licking her lips. He had a different view of these angels now that he had had his own encounters. They were not lovers. They do not love. They seduce, go through a routine of motions, and then get paid. In a sense they are like nurses, who give the required amount of care, and then quickly disappear behind the curtain.

Get back to business, you crazy sumbitch Russian. Yes, okay, I will call out to these partners to see if they have any more angels in tent.

"Obed, Alexander, are you in there? Is it safe to come in?"

Alexander answered. "That you, Bill? Come in."

Russian Bill entered the tent. "Last time I come in here there was fallen angel leaving same time. She smile at me and lick her lips in seducing manner."

Alexander laughed. "Yes, they do that, Bill. I guess it's a form of advertising."

Russian Bill studied Alexander for a moment. "You don't, uh, give yourself reward for success like Obed?"

"No, Bill, I don't. My rewards come from Mother Nature when she shows me signs that there's something of value down below."

Russian Bill handed him a small bundle of papers. "Here are your new registrations. Please give to Obed any which are his alone and for his own partnerships."

Alexander smiled. "Yes, I will do that. Thanks."

Russian Bill paused, then blurted out, "You know Bulldog mine deal I have with Mr. Hamilton C. McComas?"

"Yes. I hear that's a solid investment."

"It is more than solid, Alexander. Mr. Mc-Comas himself told me that ore from Bulldog assays over 1800 ounces of silver to the ton."

Alexander Stevensen scratched his head. "That is phenomenal, Bill. Almost unheard of. I assume he's buying all the adjacent claims."

"Oh, yes, already," Russian Bill said. "I have fifty percent interest in Sunset mine, right next to Bulldog. But I now wish to liquidate some or all of my holdings here. Do you think you and Obed might wish to acquire? I am thinking of making big change, but don't know what yet. So you make me good price for deals we have together for to buy me out. For McComas mines, I have twenty-five percent of Bulldog. Mr. McComas says this is the one we have been waiting for, so I need extra good price. I wish to sell my interest in both McComas mines as a package. I will take twelve thousand for these two in addition to our other deals. But I want the money by Friday."

"Forty-eight hours isn't much time, but I think I can do it. Are you sure you know what you're doing, Bill?"

"Thank you, Alexander. I know exactly

what I am doing."
"All right then."

CHAPTER 63

Dan Tucker was smaller than average and soft-spoken, but there was something about his eyes that could look right into your soul if you were breaking a law or disturbing the peace. Harvey Whitehill, the sheriff of Grant County, New Mexico Territory, a large area of land that contained Silver City, Deming, Lordsburg, and Shakespeare, noticed those eyes. The rest of the interview for deputy sheriff was short, over whiskeys in one of Silver City's finest saloons. Dan Tucker disclosed that he was born in Canada and that he had killed a man in Colorado. He was not a wanted man, and he was experienced with a gun. Sheriff Whitehill did not need to hear more. He knew a gunman when he saw one, and Dan Tucker was the real deal.

It was important to Sheriff Whitehill to have a town tamer work under him. Silver City was beginning to acquire a bad reputation, and that wasn't good for business or his own career. Lately there had been numerous saloon brawls, stabbings, shootings, robberies and even a gang of murderers who framed renegade Apaches as the perpetrators of the gang's own crimes.

Dan Tucker went to work right away. He killed a man who would not quit resisting during an arrest. Then he killed a man who had just cut up an enemy. Then he shot, but didn't kill, a soldier who was so drunk he no longer understood how to stop being rowdy. His next victims were horse thieves. He shot and killed two and wounded a third.

When it seemed like Silver City was settling down some, Deming, to the south, was experiencing a surge of unbridled lawlessness. Sheriff Whitehill and Deputy Dan Tucker rode down to see if they could help. In short time Dan Tucker shot and killed a man who was shooting up the town. Then he used his shotgun on a man who rode his horse into the depot and frightened a group of ladies. He found the rider out on the street and ordered the man to put his hands up. Instead the man reached down where his guns were, and that decision cost him his life.

It became widely known throughout Grant County that Dan Tucker was fearless in making an arrest or when facing an armed opponent.

Right about then is when he traveled down to Shakespeare to consult with Jackson Price and the Shakespeare Guard over the building of the new jail.

CHAPTER 64

Sandy King was originally from Kansas. He made his way to the first big silver strike in Shakespeare when he was in his twenties, and he worked for the mine owners as an enforcer during the first Shakespeare silver boom in the early 1870s. Up in Silver City, he served time for murder.

Later he rode to Tombstone and fell in with Curly Bill Brocius and the Clanton brothers. He made his way through life by rustling cattle, committing robberies, and living the high life around the saloons and gambling halls in southeastern Arizona and throughout New Mexico.

When Russian Bill had first come to Charleston in search of Curly Bill, it was Sandy King who rode up and down the street shooting his guns and causing damage to most of the buildings in town. No one was killed in the onslaught, but one random shot almost snuffed out Russian

Bill's candle as evidenced by a blown-away section of fringe from the left side of his buckskin shirt. Russian Bill had crawled to a back door and made his escape into the warm and quiet desert night, but Sandy King ended up sleeping in his own vomit, after getting knocked off his horse with a long board of lumber. Not only did he wake up with a massive headache, but his guns and money were missing.

Not content to dwell in one place while the seasons changed around him, Sandy King made the rounds to the different mining towns, ranches, and outlaw hangouts. Lately he had been drinking and raising a ruckus in all of Shakespeare's saloons. He was warned to settle down, and he finally did. That's when he started rubbing his neck. He instantly realized that his sensitive skin was chafed and burned, as it had been many times before, from countless hours of riding in the sun. He needed a neck scarf, a large one at that, and definitely silk so it wouldn't rub.

Sandy King walked from Tim Black's saloon, across the street and down the block to the general merchandise store, ignoring everyone he saw on the journey and thinking only about why he hadn't done something about this before, when he first knew that he had a problem.

"Where are your neck scarves, sonny?" he said to the young clerk in the store.

The clerk explained that it was his job to bring them out and show them to his customers, and he asked if there was a particular color he had in mind.

Sandy King pointed to his neck. "I want one with some flare. Something big to protect my neck from sunburn, and it's got to be silk. Now go ahead and bring me some."

"Yes, sir," said the clerk, and he walked over to a different part of the store where he gathered up a few neatly folded neck scarves on a shelf. By the time he had reached that shelf, he had forgotten the particulars of what his customer had specified. He brought a few neck scarves back and began showing them to his customer.

Immediately Sandy King became loud and insulting. "What is wrong with you, boy? Are you plumb weak north of the ears? These ain't what I asked for. These here are too small, they ain't silk, and they sure as shit ain't got no flare."

"Please pardon me, sir. My best friend is getting married tonight. Guess I'm thinking too much on that."

Sandy King frowned. "Then get with it,

sonny. You're movin' slower'n a snail on crutches. It's a scarf I'm wanting, not a ranch or a horse."

The young clerk walked back to the shelves where he found the first group of scarves. He opened a drawer and rummaged through the contents. Sandy King leaned against a counter and fidgeted impatiently. The clerk came back with two colorful scarves. He spread them out on the counter. "These seem to be the only ones like what you described, sir."

Sandy King chose one that had a combination of bright red and royal-blue swirls, and tied it around his neck. "Where's your glass?" he said.

The young clerk pointed. "The closest one is on that post there."

Sandy looked this way and that in the mirror. He tilted his head to the right, then stood up tall and tilted his hat to the left. Then he walked back to the young clerk. "Okay, sonny, I'll take this one. How much do ya gotta get for it?"

"Forty-nine cents, sir," said the young clerk.

"Forty-nine cents? Why that is robbery!"

The clerk was daydreaming and stuck his hand out for the money. In a fit of rage, Sandy King pulled a gun and shot off about half of the young clerk's index finger on the hand that was reaching out. The young clerk was startled by the boom. He jumped back and stared at his bloodied hand. He did not cry out, but watched the blood for a few seconds. Then he collapsed on the floor.

Sandy King, with the colorful scarf around his neck, quickly made his exit. He vaulted onto his horse but neglected to untie it from the hitching rail. He tugged, but the leather wouldn't unhitch. He was forced to climb down and unhitch it, and mount up again.

The postmaster, J. E. Long, ran out of the store as Sandy King started riding up the street. He yelled, "Stop Sandy King! He shot the young clerk and stole merchandise. He's getting away! Stop him!"

Sandy King spurred his horse and yelled, "Heyah!"

In the middle of town, outside the butcher shop, Jackson Price was speaking to Silver City Deputy Sheriff Dan Tucker about the jail they were soon to build, when they heard the shouts from the postmaster. Sure enough, here came Sandy King charging up Avon Street. Dan Tucker pulled his pistol and steadied it. As Sandy King raced by, Dan Tucker fired once, the shot knocking King off his horse.

"Great shot, Dan," said Jackson Price, the

mining superintendent and captain of the Shakespeare Guard. "Help me tie his hands and let's get the son of a bitch over to the meat locker. Too bad we don't have the new jail yet."

CHAPTER 65

John Phillips polished the boots he would wear that night at his wedding. He used his own mixture of wax, tallow, and black dye he got at the general merchandise store. He used a small brush to carefully cover the foot, heel, and shaft with the mixture. Then he rubbed it in with a rag. As he rubbed, he thought about his enchanting bride to be, Jessie Woods. The darling of all the miners and everyone else. She had chosen him, John Phillips, a store clerk. She would soon be his darling and no one else's.

As he began brushing the boots, he wondered what qualities he possessed that would make Jessie want to spend the rest of her life with him. He wasn't charming. He wasn't experienced in the area of romance. Jessie was the first girl he had ever really had a lengthy conversation with. Those were the negatives.

There must be some positives. Yes, her

mother liked him. That Anna Woods was a strong woman, and a strong influence in her daughter's life. It was she who got rid of that crazy Russian gunman. John Phillips knew that Jessie had been attracted to that Buffalo Bill lookalike. After all, he was handsome, good with a gun, obviously brave, as he did not hesitate, even after getting shot, to go after the man who killed her brother. Maybe it was the whole package that she had liked.

But he was like all other gunmen, and maybe not so different from that trouble-making cowboy who injured his friend. Shot his finger right off. For what — the price of a neck scarf?

That man was in Nick Hughes's meat locker, and the Russian had not been seen in Shakespeare for several months, thanks to the very wisdom and firmness of Anna Woods. And now he, John Phillips, would be the one to marry the beautiful Jessie tonight.

He would be a faithful husband. He would not flirt with other women or go to saloons. He did not drink or gamble. He considered drinking and gambling foolish activities. He thought of himself as fairly intelligent. He could sell things to people. Yes, he had the salesman's knack. And he was honest, unlike all those others who came knocking on Jessie's door. He would be there for her. He would be a good father to the children they would have together. He would always love her.

But would she always love him?

CHAPTER 66

The wedding of Jessie Woods and John Phillips was under way in the lobby of the Stratford Hotel. About twenty guests were seated on wooden chairs arranged in rows. Among the guests were Jackson Price, Dan Tucker, Amanda Ownby, Madge Ownby, Nora Ownby, and J. E. Long. Jessie Woods and John Phillips faced the justice of the peace, Phineas Brooks. Mrs. Anna Woods stood at Jessie's side, and the young clerk, with one hand wrapped up in bandages, stood next to John Phillips.

Russian Bill stood back where the lobby was dark. He could see and hear, but nobody noticed him. In his cover his fingers alternated from his hair to some of the remaining fringe on his shirt to his guns.

The young clerk shifted from one foot to the other and kept looking at his bandaged hand.

Phineas Brooks read from a Bible. "So the

Lord God caused a deep sleep to fall upon the man, and while he slept took one of his ribs and closed up its place with flesh. And the rib that the Lord God had taken from the man he made into a woman and brought her to the man. Then the man said, 'This at last is bone of my bones and flesh of my flesh; she shall be called woman, because she was taken out of man.' Therefore a man shall leave his father and his mother and hold fast to his wife, and they shall become one flesh."

He closed the book with a look of satisfaction and continued the ceremony. "We are gathered here today to celebrate the joining of these two young people, Jessie Woods and John Phillips, in holy matrimony. If anybody has any objections over these young people taking their vows, they better speak up now or keep their traps forever shut."

He smiled and paused for a few seconds, looking around the room. Then he continued. "Do you, John . . ."

Russian Bill stepped forward into the light. "Yes, I have objection," he said.

Several gasps were heard. Jessie Woods whirled around to face Russian Bill, a tear forming in her eye. John Phillips and the young clerk looked at each other in amazement.

Mrs. Anna Woods said, "Mr. Tettenborn! How dare you come in here at this time."

Russian Bill smiled. "Oh, I dare, Mrs. Woods. Compared to other things I've done in the past few months it is easy for me to dare. But there is nothing to worry about. I have something to say, and then I leave so wedding may continue in peace."

Jackson Price and Dan Tucker stood up. Dan Tucker pulled his coat back to reveal a silver star on his vest.

Russian Bill addressed the wedding. "A lawman is here, all the way from Silver City. Nice to see you again, Mr. Deputy Sheriff. And distinguished gentleman from Shakespeare Guard. How lovely. May I please remind lawman that preacher called for any objection. I spoke only at that time. I am keeping voice calm and will not cause alarm or trouble, only for brief comments for my objection."

Jessie Woods stared at Russian Bill, tears streaming down her face.

Russian Bill continued. "Jessie and John, I hope you have happy life together. I have gift for you here. One thousand dollars in gold. Mrs. Woods and deputy sheriff, I earned this money in legal way by investing and trading in silver mines here in Shakespeare and in Stonewall district. I would rather give gift privately at reception, but somehow I am not invited."

He paused and looked around. Mrs. Anna Woods glared at Dan Tucker for not putting a stop to this unseemly interruption.

Russian Bill pulled on his mustache. "The greatest poet, who your town is named for, expressed an idea about love in his play, *Two Gentlemen from Verona,* when he said, *They do not love that do not show their love.* Always remember to show love to each other, and do every day nice things to show love."

He paused again and patted his guns. "If I ever hear that you, John Phillips, raised angry hand or hurt Jessie in some other way, I will come look for you and possibly do something that deputy sheriff won't like. Then we have problem. Only wish for Jessie's happiness."

He paused again for the final time and held up bag of gold. "*Da svidania.* Good luck. Oh, and Mrs. Anna Woods, you are *suka* so go *po'shyol'no hui.* This is wedding present. Everyone knows that John Phillips have good head for business. Here is enough money to open store or build house, or get in big poker game. Or maybe all of that. Here, Mr. Deputy Sheriff, catch."

He tossed the bag of gold to Dan Tucker.

"Give to bride and groom after wedding, please."

He turned and walked out of the wedding ceremony, out of the Stratford Hotel and into the night, which had suddenly turned chilly.

CHAPTER 67

It was Saturday night, and business was brisk at the Roxy Jay Saloon. Cowboys, miners, businessmen and fallen angels were drinking, carousing, telling high tales, and just having a spirited time.

Russian Bill peeked inside. He took a tremendous swallow from a near-empty whiskey bottle and leaned against the wall for support. His white, fringed buckskins were tattered and filthy. A bullet hole decorated his white hat. His flowing, yellow hair that he had taken so much pride in keeping clean and neatly arranged was greasy and disheveled. His fine-leather boots were scuffed and dusty. One of them had a small hole through the instep.

He shoved open the swinging doors and stood at the entrance until the conversations ceased and all eyes were on him. He growled, "I am mangy wolf from Bitter Creek. I eat raw bear meat and stew from wildcats. I smell like dozen skunks. I weigh thousand pounds and sound of bullets whizzing by my head is favorite music."

There was an awkward stillness in the room. Then a gruff miner standing at the bar snickered. Another man howled like a wolf. Immediately everyone began laughing and returning to their previous conversations and activities.

Russian Bill tried again in a louder, drunker voice. "I am disappointed. I thought ten of you would jump up and fight. Well, that's okay. Have it your way!"

He hurled the bottle against a wall and yelled, "Watch out by door!"

He pulled a gun and blasted three holes in the already well-perforated dividing door to the gambling room. The crowd hushed and turned to watch. "Go to hell all you Shakespeare sumbitches!" This time he emptied the remainder of his gun, and the full six shots of his other pistol, into the full-length bar mirror, shattering it and sending shards flying. Frightened and bewildered patrons dove for cover, some spilling drinks and yelling obscenities.

Russian Bill ran outside and jumped on his big, white horse. As he began to ride, the Roxy Jay bartender scrambled outside with a rifle and fired off one round. The white horse collapsed, sending Russian Bill sprawling, his wind temporarily knocked out.

He crawled back to the horse and lifted its head, stroking it with trembling hands. He quietly said, "I never tell you how much I love you. I give you plenty hard work, and you are best horse in whole world. Where you go now I don't know, but maybe I will meet you again soon."

He loaded two cartridges in his gun. One he fired in the general direction of the Roxy Jay bartender, sending him scampering back inside the saloon. Then he placed the gun barrel against his own temple, and, still stroking the horse's head, he closed his eyes. He held that way for a few seconds, and then jammed the gun back into its holster while muttering something in Russian. He quickly removed pouches of gold, a blanket roll, and canteen from the up side of the dead horse. He crawled to a hitching rail and secured his belongings on the one horse that had turned to watch him approach, a handsome black. Once in the saddle, he spurred it and galloped out of town as Avon Street began to fill with spectators.

CHAPTER 68

The black horse was game all right, but was shorter and had a slightly different gait. Russian Bill noticed that his boot heels were closer to the ground. After considering the options, Russian Bill had decided to take the road north. He would make his way to the mining camps of Colorado. He could get new buckskin clothing up there. Maybe he would visit Buffalo Bill and tell him how many times he had been called by that name. Yes, there would be many stories to tell Buffalo Bill.

He might resume speculating on mines. He learned a great deal from his associations with Obed Foote and Alexander Stevensen, with Hamilton McComas, and from so many others. While he might not be able to recognize many rocks and minerals, he could certainly identify ore that contained silver, gold or copper. He felt confident that he could hold his own with the best of mine speculators.

As he rode, his thoughts turned to the wedding. How plain and simple it was, not like any of the weddings he had attended in his country, with pageantry and decorations and food and drink. And the receptions lasted all through the night, not just shake the groom's hand and kiss the bride on the cheek, and then it's over.

A large buck dashed across the road and bounded away. That jolted Russian Bill's nerves and caused him to sit up straight in the saddle. There was a little more than a quarter moon. The road could be seen, but there were all kinds of dangers out there. He needed to pay attention to his surroundings.

He had been riding for hours. The left side of his body was still very sore, and he knew that riding long distances would not be conducive to proper healing. His foot also throbbed. It was a good time to allow the black horse to walk. It would not be likely that anyone would come after him this night. He would find a place to take a short nap, and then head north. He would buy a new horse and arrange for someone to return this black one to its rightful owner in Shakespeare with a small purse of gold coins for the trouble.

There would have to be a payment for the Roxy Jay's bar glass he shot up. But wait, that sumbitch bartender shot and killed his horse. That made it about even, didn't it? The bar glass was very special. It took eighteen mules to cart it for the last twenty miles. And wasn't the big, white horse special too? Didn't it get attention everywhere it went? Didn't people always want to buy it or trade for it? Yes indeed, they were even, all right.

And what of Jessie? Now she is married. Didn't she look even more beautiful in that white dress? But for what were the tears? Were they because her special day was ruined? Or was there another reason, a more personal reason? He decided that he would never know.

CHAPTER 69

Dan Tucker and Jackson Price rode at a moderate clip as they tracked Russian Bill north through the western New Mexico desert. Dan Tucker said, "That crazy sumbitch is not trying to hide his tracks."

Jackson Price cautioned, "We better stay alert then. He could be hiding where he can murder us as we ride."

Every time they reached a stand of boulders or a hill, Jackson Price got nervous. Dan Tucker calmed him down and told him why that particular spot was not a good hiding place. On the last stand of low boulders they approached, they could see for at least a mile in every direction and there had been no place for Russian Bill to hide the stolen horse.

Dan Tucker stopped again to look at the tracks in the dirt. He seemed like he was in no hurry, and his attitude was that nobody he was tracking could ever get away. So he frequently got out of the saddle, walked his horse, drank water from his canteen, ate a biscuit, and relieved himself in the sand.

Jackson Price admired Dan Tucker's nerve, but found it difficult to carry on that way. Actually he was tired. He was not used to riding that far. He climbed down and walked his horse, stretching his legs. He, too, ate a biscuit while walking and took a drink from his own canteen. He secretly wished that all of this tracking was over and he was back in Shakespeare.

Dan Tucker followed their man to a place near Deming where the new railroad tracks had recently been laid. Two boxcars were the only structures in the vicinity, apparently used as storage.

The door on the first boxcar was closed. The other door was open slightly. Dan Tucker cautiously stuck his head inside while Jackson Price poked around outside.

Dan Tucker pulled one of his guns. "He's in there sound asleep and snoring."

Jackson Price wiped his forehead with a bandana. "Robert Hart's horse is around back."

Dan Tucker slid the boxcar door open all the way. He yelled, "Wake your ass up, Tettenborn. Stick your hands high in the air or I'll have no trouble blowing you away right here right now."

CHAPTER 70

Three riders headed back to Shakespeare. Russian Bill, with hands tied in front with strips of cloth, and feet bound underneath Robert Hart's horse, was sandwiched between Jackson Price and Dan Tucker.

Russian Bill was silent for most of the ride, absorbed in his own thoughts. How had he allowed himself to oversleep like that? That extra sleep just might bring forth the really big sleep. The forever sleep. Curly Bill had advised him at the end of his recuperation in the Willcox boardinghouse. *And this is the most important rule because it can cost you your life. Don't ever ride another man's horse without his permission. Even touching another man's horse is almost as bad as touching his wife. Always remember that out here a horse thief pays with his life.*

Perhaps he should find out if his captors were open to a good bribe. "Hey, Mr. Deputy Sheriff and Mr. Shakespeare

Guards, I have lot of money buried in secret locations in sand. This money is legal earned. I heard that you want to build jail. How about we make deal. I pay for jail. I pay for very nice jail for Shakespeare. Better than the flea-ridden, cracker-box jail in Tombstone. Then I pay owner of horse I borrowed because bartender at Roxy Jay's shot and killed my own beautiful horse. I gladly will pay him premium money for inconvenience. You gentlemen have also been put out. I am prepared to pay you both large sum of money to allow me to escape. No one else knows that you have me captured. You can say whatever you want and still have very much money. And you can take horse back to owner. All I will need is some water . . ."

"Shut up!" Dan Tucker yelled. "You can't buy us. I don't give a shit what they do to you in Shakespeare, but I'm gonna see that you get there."

The way Russian Bill's feet were tied under the horse, he had difficulty with any kind of shifting in the saddle, and the entire left side of his body ached, as well as his lower back and his foot from the bullet wound.

Russian Bill looked at Dan Tucker. He thought that he understood that deputy. An opposite from Johnny Behan's deputy, Dan Tucker enjoyed being in charge and fearless. Billy Breakenridge was not like that. He ate too much, and he read books. Curly Bill could well have advised Deputy Breakenridge that he was too well educated to be a member of Johnny Behan's posse. But this Dan Tucker. He was a force, a shooting star here on the earthly desert. Russian Bill realized that he would not be released, and, once he reached Shakespeare, it would be too late to receive any help or consideration.

A hawk high above rode the air currents and screamed a lonely, piercing note as it looked down upon the three men riding side by side. Russian Bill glanced up and smiled. Though he was unable to shield his eyes from the bright sun, he saw the solitary hawk soaring and envied that bird its freedom.

When the trio of riders arrived in Shakespeare, Jackson Price led them to a boardinghouse where he knew that meals could be obtained at all hours. Jackson Price dismounted and untied Russian Bill's feet from underneath the horse. When he slid out of the saddle, Jackson Price retied his feet, so it was necessary for him to shuffle in order to move. In this tedious manner, he followed his captors into the boarding-house.

In the dining room the men sat at a large table. A middle-aged widow, Mrs. Whittle-sea, entered the room. Russian Bill stood up for a moment, then sat back down. Dan Tucker motioned for attention. "Bring us three dinners. Make sure Buffalo Bill over here gets something he won't have to cut up because he won't be using any kind of knife."

Russian Bill smiled and, with hands tied in the front, reached up to tip his hat to the woman. She smiled back and exited to the kitchen. Dan Tucker and Jackson Price did not speak.

In a jiffy Mrs. Whittlesea returned with a tray containing napkins and cutlery, a basket of warm biscuits, coffee and water. She distributed them, spending extra time with Russian Bill, who tasted one of the warm biscuits and told her that she was most kind, and that he was certain he had never tasted a better biscuit in his entire life.

A short time later a hearty beef-stew dinner was served, with more hot biscuits. Russian Bill struggled but managed to use the fork to shovel food in his mouth. When the main course was finished Mrs. Whittlesea

303

asked Dan Tucker if dessert was wanted. She started to explain about the special apple pie that had come out of her oven only two hours earlier. Jackson Price shook his head and set some money on the table. He and Dan Tucker used their sleeves to wipe their mouths. Russian Bill used the cloth napkin from his lap.

Dan Tucker stood up. "Get up, Tettenborn. Time to go."

Russian Bill stood up and looked at Mrs. Whittlesea. "Thank you, ma'am. That was awesome meal. Thank you for hospitality."

Mrs. Whittlesea smiled warmly at Russian Bill, ignoring the other men.

CHAPTER 71

A prospector and member of the Shakespeare Guards named Sam Ransom sat outside Nick Hughes's meat market, his hat brim tilted low over his forehead, a Winchester rifle in his hands. He had been appointed to guard Sandy King, who was locked up inside the meat locker, and he was feeling important. Sam knew there was only one way out of that meat locker. The only possible threat would come from the street, but even that wouldn't be likely as the prisoner had not murdered anyone, but only raised a ruckus and shot the finger off of a young clerk. He had been told to check on the prisoner once or twice, but had elected not to do that. The sumbitch inside could rot in hell as far as he was concerned, and why take any chances with a wily outlaw?

It was early evening when the trio of riders stopped directly in front of him. Jackson

Price smiled and said, "Open up, Sam. We got the Russian."

As Sam Ransom stood up, straightened out his hat, and fumbled with some keys, Robert Hart ran over from across the street. "That's my horse, you Russian piece of shit scum bastard sumbitch horse thief! You have no idea who you were thieving from when you unhitched that horse, Mr. big-talking Russian prince. Now you're gonna see what we do to horse thieves and bottom dwellers here in Shakespeare."

Jackson Price untied Russian Bill's feet and helped him slide off the black horse. Dan Tucker had a gun leveled at his heart. Robert Hart took his horse from Jackson Price and looked it over. Then Robert Hart backhanded Russian Bill across the face, knocking his white hat into the street.

Russian Bill smiled and took one small step in Robert Hart's direction. "Boo!" he yelled, sending Hart sprawling awkwardly backwards.

"You'll see," Robert Hart said emotionally as he retreated with his horse.

A crowd began to form as several saloons emptied from the shouting at the meat market. Dan Tucker said, "Better get this sumbitch put away quick."

Sam Ransom found what he thought was

the right key and attempted to open the meat-market door. But the key was wrong and just turned around and around in the door lock.

"Better give them to me, Sam," Jackson Price said, reaching for the ring of keys. The first one he tried clicked, and he was able to open the door. Dan Tucker followed Jackson Price and Russian Bill inside the store. At the end of the service counter, the metal meat-locker door was opened by Jackson Price. Then Russian Bill was roughly shoved inside by Dan Tucker. The door was slammed and the outside lock was set in place. Immediately the door was opened again and Russian Bill's white hat was thrown inside.

Outside, Jackson Price told Sam Ransom to continue guarding the door. If there was any trouble, he should fire his rifle in the air.

Then he addressed the crowd of about two dozen men who had gathered in the street. "Nothing's gonna happen here tonight. You men should go home or go about your business. We've been riding all day and need some rest. We'll deal with the prisoners soon. Everything's under our control now, so go on now and leave the area."

Russian Bill instantly felt chilled as his

eyes adjusted to the semi-darkness, and his lungs adjusted to the dank odor of beef, pork, venison and poultry carcasses hanging from hooks or laid out on racks and shelves. A single oil lamp hung on a wall hook and provided the only light in the cold and damp enclosure.

Sandy King sat against the back wall. When Russian Bill noticed him, he made his way over and slid down the wall beside him. "You are Sandy King? You shoot fringe off shirt, nearly kill me one night in Charleston, long time ago, when you shoot up town. I did not understand that behavior then, but now I do. I shoot sacred mirror all to hell in Roxy Jay's, then steal horse of important man in Shakespeare Guards. They catch me when I take nap in railroad train car used for storage near new section of tracks by Deming. Was supposed to take catnap, but oversleep and now I am here with you. Is it true you shoot finger off store clerk?"

Sandy King nodded. "Listen, I ain't in no mood for chitchat. I'm colder than a Minnesota well-digger in December. They shot me off my horse and the ball is still in my arm. My hands is tied behind my back, so I can't even scratch my nuts. I ain't et in I dunno how long. I need a drink real bad and they won't even let me take a piss. So you can see why I don't feel sociable."

Russian Bill slid a few feet down the wall away from Sandy King. "I'm sorry to disturb. I will be quiet now."

There was silence for a time, but then Russian Bill couldn't stand it any longer. He blurted out, "Did you ever ride horse with feet tied underneath and hands tied in front? That's how I ride all the way from Deming. Plus I got shot in foot right through boot, got knocked off moving train and fall off horse in Indian attack. I don't need to scratch nuts. They are too sore to scratch from saddle bounce without ability to shift position."

He paused again for a few minutes. Then he said, "You, Sandy King, have many disabilities right now. You have right to feel sorry for yourself. But so do I. In addition to all my aches and pains and the indignities I went through and will continue to go through, I witnessed the wedding of the girl I love to other man."

Russian Bill got quiet again. Soon enough though his thoughts got the better of him. "So you don't want to talk, good for you. Go fuck yourself. I can get by okay fine talking to myself."

For quite some time Russian Bill spoke to

himself silently. He thought that Sandy King should have embraced him at a time like this. They were fellow prisoners, comrades. Once again, he was in a situation where he was not worthy of being a part of the outlaw fraternity. Once again, perhaps for the final time in his life, he was rejected.

Russian Bill began shivering. He had not felt that kind of chill in his bones since living in St. Petersburg in the winter. He glanced at Sandy King. He was sitting still, staring straight ahead into the carcasses, with his eyes half-closed. He was not shivering. *Bet he would talk if Curly Bill was here. Or John Ringo. Or even that kid, Jim Hughes.*

A scraping sound was heard, then the door opened and a storm of light illuminated the hanging carcasses. Russian Bill shuddered. *They have come for me and Sandy King,* he thought. *Now they will take me some place and I will soon be just like these animals.* But the noise was not of an angry mob, or even of Jackson Price or Dan Tucker.

It was Jim Hughes, with his hands and feet tied, giggling drunk. "Hello, boys," he said, as he hopped by the carcasses over to where they sat.

CHAPTER 72

Jim Hughes slumped down next to Russian Bill. The door shut and the lock slid into place. Russian Bill smiled. "What did you do, more horse trading?"

"No, I got drunk. Some big miners, with strange foreign accents — no offense, Bill — started messing with me. I made 'em dance and shot up the saloon. Not the one you mutilated. I shot up Tim Black's place. How was I supposed to know Tim is in the Shakespeare Guards?"

Russian Bill said, "I know what you mean. I make same mistake. They kill my beautiful, white horse, so I take another. I don't realize it belonged to another person in Guards. I was in hurry and upset and did not stop to ask questions. Just untie horse and scram out of town."

Jim Hughes shifted position to try to get more comfortable. "Sure is whiffy in here. What's with Sandy King? He ain't moved an inch since I got here."

Russian Bill tugged at the cloth restraints to try to free his hands, but they would not budge. "He's not in the mood for chitchat, because he is shot in arm and can't scratch nuts, he's hungry and needs a drink, and they won't let him take piss."

Sandy King turned his face and scowled at Russian Bill. "I wish I could just free my one good arm so's I could pummel this foreign sumbitch's voice box to shut him up. I tell you I can't stand his voice anymore."

Russian Bill smiled. "Maybe we will have a chance to settle disagreements one day when your other arm is healed and I am recovered."

Sandy King chuckled. "Don't you get it? There ain't gonna be no chances to heal or recover. These boys mean to string us up. Make examples of us. They been waiting a long time for this opportunity."

Russian Bill said, "Why they do that? We don't kill anyone. Maybe they fine us and make us leave town. What do you think, Jim Hughes?"

"I think they will just try to scare us is all."

Sandy King shifted positions and winced in pain. "I'm so miserable right now, I wish they'd just hang me and get it over with."

Russian Bill wanted to change the subject, and he turned to Jim Hughes. "Isn't this your father's meat store?"

Jim Hughes smiled. "It sure is. Funny thing is, he used to threaten that he'd lock me up in here when I mouthed off to him or didn't listen. I never imagined that this would be used as a jail and I'd be one of the first prisoners in it."

Russian Bill said, "Won't your father try to help you out of jam?"

Jim Hughes smiled. "Naw. Me and him don't exactly get along. When he finds out what happened and why I'm in here, he'll be mad enough to kick his own dog. My ma loves me, though. How long have y'all been here?"

"I don't know if it's been minutes, hours or maybe a day," said Russian Bill. "Sandy King was already here when I make entrance."

"How long you been in here, Sandy?" Jim Hughes asked.

"Long enough to want to kill somebody or have somebody kill me. I don't much care which." After saying this he went back to staring straight ahead, almost as if he were in a silent trance.

Jim Hughes slid all the way down and

went to sleep.

Russian Bill was achy and weary, but not sleepy. He let his thoughts take over. First he was back in Russia walking through St. Petersburg in the winter snow. His hair was short and he wore a red officer's uniform. Then he was fighting with another officer. They rolled through the snow punching and kicking. When Russian Bill grabbed at his own bloodied nose, the other officer pulled a gun. Russian Bill lunged and grabbed the hand that held that weapon. The gun discharged and the air filled with smoke.

He imagined fighting both Dan Tucker and Sandy King, but they rolled around in the desert sand. His gun discharged twice in his mind, and both Tucker and King were killed. He picked up a shovel to dig holes to bury these men, but suddenly he had a thought.

He brought two wild coyotes, one in each arm, over to the two bodies and set them down.

They immediately began consuming the dead men.

Then he went back into the Stratford Hotel. His white buckskins were immaculate again and there was no hole in either his clean, white hat or his polished, black boots. He called out, *Oh, Mrs. Anna Woods. Come*

here, please. I have something special for you.
Mrs. Woods came into the dining room, and Russian Bill blew her away with a shotgun.

He then led a bear into the Stratford with a rope and pointed to the bloodied corpse on the dining-room floor.

The big, white horse was doing tricks for children near the community well at Lookout Point on the edge of town.

Russian Bill leaped onto Jim Wallace and shot him through the neck. Then he jumped Bean Belly Smith and shot him though the belly.

Next came Jackson Price. Russian Bill used the shotgun to blow his kneecaps out.

Then the Roxy Jay bartender and a dozen men were unloading the huge replacement mirror from an eighteen-mule wagon. Russian Bill unloaded both guns into the new mirror, then he picked up the shotgun and used both barrels on the bartender.

Russian Bill was awakened by a scraping sound. At last, someone was coming to take the three prisoners out of the freezing, stinking room.

Chapter 73

The first Shakespeare Guard entered the meat locker with a rifle. He looked around nervously at the meat carcasses hanging. Then he spotted the three prisoners along the back wall. "All right, you sumbitches," he said with false authority. "You're coming with me. Get up." He took four steps forward, and then slipped in a pool of blood from the carcasses. He went down hard and slid all the way into the back wall, his rifle falling loose and sliding right to the feet of Sandy King. Sandy King used his feet to pick up the rifle and position it between his knees, barrel out.

"I ain't got no hands, but I'm still gonna shoot you in the eye, you miserable sumbitch guard. Wouldn't feed me nothing or even let me take a piss? You don't even treat dogs in this manner. Here I go; I'm gonna shoot you now, you hear me?"

The guard slipped around on the floor,

but then his boots found some traction, and he ran out the door and quickly closed it.

Sandy King started laughing. "That fool believed that I could shoot this thing without using my hands. At least I had one last hurrah. That was the most fun I've ever had without the aid of liquor."

Jim Hughes shook his head. "But did you ever think that they might now come in here blasting?"

Sandy King was all smiles. "I hope they do. I have no hankering for dangling on the end of a rope."

The door opened again and Jackson Price walked in with four other men. He looked at Sandy King. "You can just drop that rifle now, Sandy. We're all gonna go for a little wagon ride. Get the rifle, Patrick. You other men, help those others up and let's march them out of here."

When Sandy King was grabbed by the arm he screamed and cursed the guard for touching the arm that still held Dan Tucker's bullet. Jim Hughes and Russian Bill were taken quietly out of the temporary jail and into the warm night.

Russian Bill instantly felt the rush of soothing, warm air. He still had the horrid dead animal smell in his nose though, and wondered if it would yield to the pleasing smells of mesquite firewood burning in the homes and restaurants in the town. Meanwhile the Shakespeare Guards standing with rifles and torches in the street presented an eerie and frightening sight.

The three prisoners still had their hands and feet bound. They were poked with rifle barrels and told to hop over to the wagon. Then they leaned back and received assistance in swinging their legs into the wagon for the short ride to the Grant House Stagecoach Station. Although it was only a distance of forty yards, they never would have been able to make it there unless their feet were untied. That would present a security problem. Jackson Price had suggested the wagon, and no one had objected.

The wagon rolled slowly down Avon Street. Men with rifles and torches followed on foot. Once at the Grant House, the prisoners were helped down to the street and into the station. Once inside, they were lifted onto the long dinner table where stagecoach passengers rested and ate a meal along their journey. Crude rope nooses were placed over their heads, and the ropes were thrown over a heavy ceiling beam.

Jackson Price wasted no time in getting started. "Sandy King, you are a troublemaker and a damned nuisance. You stole that damned neck scarf and you disfigured that boy you shot. Jim Hughes, you should know better. Your parents are upstanding citizens in this community, but time after time you come to town and disturb the peace. It's just a matter of time before some innocent bystander is gonna get killed by your foolishness if we don't take action right here, right now."

Sandy King interrupted. "Boys, give me a shot of t'rantula juice to help me face the hellfire. I think you're stretching the damage I done, where other towns would have just thrown my ass in a proper jail for a few weeks. And treated me humane, too. Not like this. But that's okay. I know I've long been a sinner and don't have any grounds to kick. B'sides, kickin' never gets you nowheres lessen you're a mule."

Robert Hart got him a shot of whiskey from the bar, and, because Sandy King's hands were tied, the Shakespeare Guard stood on a chair and poured it into King's open mouth.

Then Jim Hughes spoke up. "Please boys, give me a chance. Look at me — I'm young. I can change; I swear I can. I'm like the top string of bob wire, high-strung, but I got my good points, too."

One of the Guards laughed, and Jackson

Price elbowed him.

"And how 'bout you, William Tettenborn or Russian Bill or whatever you're calling yourself today? Ever since you got here you've been blowin' dust about how many men you've killed. Frankly most folks thought you was just piling it on, but now you've destroyed a sacred institution in this town and stole Robert Hart's horse to boot."

Jackson Price paused and looked at Russian Bill, who stood silent and motionless staring straight ahead.

"Well, the citizens of Shakespeare have had enough of you. You three have harrahed the town, injured innocent folks, thieved, destroyed property and carried on like the outlaw scum that you are. You are hereby sentenced to death by hanging, and I hope that word quickly spreads that your kind needs to find another place to work their mischief."

A hundred thoughts poured through Russian Bill's consciousness. He thought of his mama back home in Russia. He thought of Jessie. Images of some of the stunts that Curly Bill had him do that showed he was not outlaw material and too much of a gentleman danced in his head. He thought of his horse dying out in the street, and how he had replaced Curly Bill's horse when Curly carelessly shot it through the boards of the Gem Saloon in Galeyville. No horse alive could ever replace his own big, white horse, and he had never even given him a name. Most of all, his thoughts went back to what he thought Jackson Price had just said. Had Russian Bill just been called *outlaw scum*? Suddenly he wasn't sure. This point was important and needed to be clarified. He said, "You gentlemen and the good citizens of Shakespeare believe that I am an outlaw scum?"

Robert Hart, who was happy enough to get his horse back but mad as hell that somebody had the gall to steal it, said, "You're damn right we do, and . . ."

Just then the door opened and two women rushed in. They were Josefa Hughes, mother of Jim Hughes, and Jessie Woods Phillips. They were both crying.

Josefa Hughes between sobs said, "Let him go! He's just a boy. I'll see he leaves town. You won't have to worry about him causing trouble ever again. Please! I beg you. If you hang that boy you'll be killing me, too. I swear it."

There was no response, so she hung her head and continued to cry. Jessie Woods Phillips hugged Russian Bill's legs and moaned quietly.

Russian Bill looked down at Jessie and smiled. "There now, Jessie darling. Do not say anything, please. You have new life now. Your husband, he seems like good man. Go to him now, please. And do not waste tears of sadness for me."

Sandy King said, "Give me another drink, boys, and I'll go to hell shouting."

Jackson Price nodded and Robert Hart got a drink from the bar. He repeated the process of feeding it to Sandy King.

"Get ready on those ropes," said Jackson Price.

Josefa Hughes screamed, "No!"

Jessie Woods Phillips said quietly, as if to herself, "Please don't do this."

Russian Bill's expression turned from one of concern to the beginning of a smile. He said, "Wait, gentlemen! Let the boy go! You want to set examples, well you have two good ones here. You don't need him."

Tim Black, who was having second thoughts about hanging the boy, said, "I'd be a hell of a lot more forgiving if someone would pay for the damages to my saloon."

Josefa Hughes said, "My husband and I will pay. Just bring me the bill."

Tim Black asked Jackson Price, "Okay with you?"

Jackson Price paced around for a minute. Then he said, "Mrs. Hughes, do you agree to pay for all damages caused by your son and arrange for his permanent relocation from Shakespeare and all of Grant County?"

Josefa Hughes said, "Yes, I do. I will."

Jackson Price said, "All right."

Robert Hart removed the noose and carried Jim Hughes off the table. He then untied his hands and feet.

Jim Hughes ran into his mother's arms. But he quickly turned and looked at Russian Bill. Russian Bill smiled at him. Jim Hughes smiled back. Josefa Hughes and Jessie Woods Phillips sobbed again.

Jackson Price said, "Let's get this over with. All right, you men, get ready on those ropes."

Russian Bill looked down at Jessie. He quietly said to her, *The stroke of death is as a lover's pinch, which hurts and is desired.*

Jackson Price yelled, "Pull!"

Three men on each rope raised Sandy King and Russian Bill. The nooses were crude and not proper hangman's knots, so the two men choked and strangled and kicked for quite some time before suffocating.

CHAPTER 74

There was a chill in the air when the Butterfield stage pulled to a dusty stop outside the Grant House station the following morning. Six tired and hungry passengers stretched their legs and entered the station to get their coffee and breakfast. Instead of finding a warm welcome, they were greeted by the bodies of two dead men still hanging from the heavy ceiling beam.

"Jesus Christ," said one of the passengers. "What happened here?"

A short man named Harry was the station master. He oversaw all passenger-related activities in the station, and his wife, a heavyset, Mexican woman, did all the cooking. Harry waited until all the passengers were inside the station. Then he said, "These men were hung last night. I am under strict orders from the Shakespeare Guards that you people are not to have your breakfast until these corpses are removed to the wagon outside. I'm afraid you will have to do it before we can serve you anything."

Another passenger said, "This is bullshit. This doesn't have anything to do with us. Why make us do it?"

Harry said, "Look, I'm just following orders. I believe their way of thinking is that this is the best way to spread the word that lawlessness will not be tolerated in Shakespeare."

Another passenger asked what these men had done to deserve this execution.

Harry scratched his bald head. "The yellow-haired one in all the fringes stole a horse. The other one was just a damned nuisance."

Russian Bill's fine boots, even though one of them had a bullet-hole breach, never made it to the wagon.

About six months after the hanging, Shakespeare's postmaster, J. E. Long, received a letter forwarded by the Russian Consul. The letter was from Countess Telfrin, a lady-in-waiting to the Czarina of Russia. It said that she had been getting regular letters from her son, William R. Tettenborn, but he suddenly stopped writing. She wanted to know if the postmaster could provide any information.

The postmaster replied, "Dear Madam, I regret to inform you that your son has died of throat trouble."

Curly Bill Brocius disappeared from Arizona and New Mexico a few months after the double hanging in Shakespeare. Wyatt Earp said that he killed him during a gunfight at Burleigh Springs in the Whetstone Mountains, but the body has never been found.

From time to time the figure of a man has been seen walking through Shakespeare in the dark of night, undisturbed by the barking of dogs. Some say this is Curly Bill, still searching for those kindly housewives that had looked after his needs for so many years.

After Curly Bill disappeared, John Ringo was found dead on a Turkey Creek ranch at the base of the Chiricahua Mountains. Some say that Wyatt Earp got him, too, but many others insist that the bullet that bored the large hole in his head was fired from his own gun, the gun that was still in his hand when his body was found leaning against a tree.

Jim Hughes left Shakespeare but continued outlaw activities in Arizona and New Mexico. He married twice and died of a liver ailment in Deming at the age of thirty-nine.

Dan Tucker died of natural causes at the age of forty-three.

Baby Mattie Johnson grew up to be a large-boned, healthy woman. She lived a full and happy life.

Jessie Woods Phillips and her husband moved to California, where they opened a store. It was very successful. On her deathbed she asked her son to scatter her ashes in Shakespeare.

After the hanging, life returned to normal in Shakespeare for quite some time. It was well over a year before a single shot was fired within the city limits, and that was a harmless accident.

The Shakespeare Guard continued to maintain law and order for generations.

The notorious outlaws Russian Bill and Sandy King rest side by side in the Shakespeare cemetery.

ABOUT THE AUTHOR

Richard Lapidus has been a teacher, a successful businessman, and a writer. His writings specialize in reptiles and the Old West. His book *Snake Hunting on the Devil's Highway* is a collection of humorous, true short stories about his adventures hunting for snakes in Arizona. His first novel, *Snakey Joe Post, Guardian of the Treasure,* is an historical novel about a man who discovers a treasure of incalculable value and wants nothing to do with it.

Richard's writings have appeared in national magazines, history, science and nature journals, newspapers, and in books by other authors.

Richard is a member of the Western Writers of America. He lives in Henderson, Nevada, with his wife of 48 years, two sons, and a granddaughter.

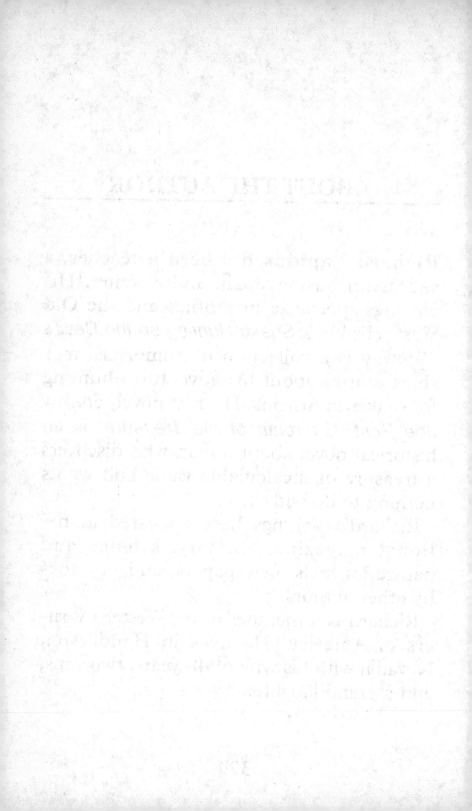

The employees of Thorndike Press hope you have enjoyed this Large Print book. All our Thorndike, Wheeler, and Kennebec Large Print titles are designed for easy reading, and all our books are made to last. Other Thorndike Press Large Print books are available at your library, through selected bookstores, or directly from us.

For information about titles, please call:
  (800) 223-1244

or visit our Web site at:
  http://gale.cengage.com/thorndike

To share your comments, please write:
  Publisher
  Thorndike Press
  10 Water St., Suite 310
  Waterville, ME 04901